Strange Occurrences

Sarah Elizabeth

DEDICATION

This book is dedicated to my family, who were so supportive
over the writing process.

CONTENTS

ACKNOWLEDGMENTS

I would like to thank all of the friends and family who helped me through writing this book. Thank you guys so much. I would especially like to thank my best friend, who put up with my constant talking about trying to write a book for years.

The Strange Girl

The wind whistled high and loud, screaming in the girl's ears as she sat down on the rubble. Dust and ash covered everything around her, and she began to sob as she looked around. She really was alone now. Where had everything gone so wrong? She had finally found a place where she belonged, after waiting so long, and now it was gone, snatched away. Hot, heavy tears rolled down her cheeks, warming her frozen cheeks which stung in the cold air. She buried her face in her hands, not knowing what else to do. What else could she do? She had lost everything now, and her heart ached.

Two months ago...

The cool fall air blew gently across the empty streets and whistled past the buildings. Leaves fell from the small trees boxed into the parks, and they swirled along the roads. The sun had begun to rise, and they city sprung to life with traffic and lights. Noise and light flooded the city, and filled the air with the thick smell of gasoline and smoke.

The first thing that Rani thought when she woke up was about how bad the apartment smelled. She was used to bad smells; Gavin, her step dad, was a heavy smoker , but it smelled bad all the same. She rolled out of bed and pulled on her clothes, a worn T-shirt, and old jeans. She pulled her hair back into a loose pony tail and pulled on her favorite loose grey sweatshirt. Gagging at the smell, she sprayed some body spray to help mask the smoke smell that clung to everything she wore.

Rani walked out into the hall and into the kitchen. Her step dad was sprawled out on the couch, an empty beer bottle hanging loosely in his hands. Three or four more were on the floor nearby. It was only two more steps to the small kitchen, where she grabbed a quick bite to eat and headed out the door. A quick elevator ride took her to the bottom of apartment building where she and her family lived.

Her apartment was small and cramped. It was hard to believe that five people lived there, six if you counted Gavin, but Rani refused to believe that he was human. He was more like some gigantic slobbery pig that someone had put clothes on. Rani could still smell the smoke when she got to the bus stop. She must not have used enough body spray, but she knew that no matter how much 'tropical breeze' body spray she put on, she couldn't get the smell of poverty and filth off of her. The bus bumped down the road, the brakes letting out a high pitched screech as it stopped. The ride to school was too short for Rani's liking, since she was buried deep in the mass of buildings, and at the heart of the city was the school. Rani was a sophomore, and it was her second year with the tough crowd from the bad parts of town. She lived in a bad part of town, but that didn't make it any easier for her to adjust to seeing thugs roaming the school halls like they owned them. She shuffled through the halls until she got to her first period class. She was like a shadow during school; no one noticed her in the bleakness of the classrooms. She liked the feeling of being invisible; she didn't feel like her old self anymore. Automatically, her fingers went to the chains around her neck. On one was a lightning bolt. A tiny inscription on the back read *I'll hold you through the storm*. It had been her father's favorite quote. He wore one just like it. He still wore it around his neck. Rani knew because the silver glint had been the last thing she had seen before they had closed the coffin lid.

The other one was a locket, with a baby picture of her sister. She had run away when she was eight, and when Rani was only four. No one spoke her name, and so Rani only knew the SAM that was carved onto the silver locket. Rani had long since given up trying to uncover her sisters name; her mom only cried when she asked. Maybe running away wasn't such a crazy idea like she had thought it was years ago. Back when she had a dad, and a nice house, running away had sounded crazy. Now, she wasn't so sure it was. Rani would do anything for a place to feel like she belonged. She wondered if her sister belonged wherever she was.

The next classes slid by slowly at a snail's pace, until Rani found herself sitting; weary, in front of a computer in the computer lab. She was mostly focused on her work. She stiffened as a group of girls walked behind her. The smell of smoke had mostly vanished now, but some still lingered, along with the smell of cheap perfume. She heard the girls stop behind her, and she pretended to be completely focused on the screen in front of her.

"Oh dear, I don't think Rani is talking to use today!" said the one, pouncing it Ray-nee instead of how it was, Rah-Nee. Rani's cheeks went red, but she focused on her computer screen.

"I wouldn't either, if I were. She's got a big mouth that one, and it only attracts attention to the rest of her." The speaker wrinkled her nose. "And we would want that, now would we?" Rani sighed and stared their reflections in the screen. *Why can't they bug someone else?* She thought to herself.

"My god, did you even try to run I comb through this," exclaimed another in disgust, extending a perfectly manicured finger towards Rani's hair. It was a soft chocolate brown, with curls spiraling halfway down her back. Rani had always thought her hair was her best feature, but listening to these girls, doubts began to swirl around her. She gripped the edge of her seat. She was used to their constant nagging by now, but it was annoying never less. Even more so that she used to be friends with most of these girls, until her mom had married Gavin. Before that, she hadn't smelled like smoke, she had nice clothes, and had friends. She had also only been nine years old, when people weren't all that mean and quick to judge.

"Poor, poor Rani" A different beautiful girl said. Rani clenched the edge of her seat. She could feel something inside her, an anger she couldn't control. She struggled to keep it down, but it was rising, bubbling over. She could feel heat rising out of the computer in front of her, and it only made her face go redder.

"Where's your dad, Rani?" said the beautiful girl. "Where is he?"

The lights in the computer lab flickered.

"Where is he?" She sneered.

The lights in the computer lab grew to blinding. Rani gulped in air and bit her lip hard. She squeezed her eyes shut. The children in the computer lab yelped. Gasps came out in surprise.

Rani had her eyes squeezed shut and had calmed her breathing. *In, out, In and out,* she thought. She opened her eyes just as the lights snapped out. In the darkness, she could make out the disbelief on her classmates faces. None of them were looking at her, though; they were staring at the ceiling. A lone tear streaked down Rani's face. She knew what waited later.

*   *   *

Rani was sitting in the room she shared with her least favorite step-sibling, Aubrey. She sat cross legged on her bed, her mom's laptop in her lap. She was once again looking for strange cases in the United States. Anything, from random windows shattering, to random lightning strikes when there was no rain. A candle was burning on the dresser, filling the room with the fresh smell of apples instead of smoke and beer. The room was small and the beds were bunk to make room for a dresser, Aubrey's, and a box, which belonged to Rani.

She heard the front door slam, and she knew that Aubrey had just arrived. Aubrey was a fat, tall girl, at least for age. She wore one size bigger than Rani in shirts, and should have been one size bigger in pants too, but she squeezed herself into skinny jeans that were meant for skinny girls like Rani. Aubrey had long hair, and small, beady eyes. She looked a lot like her dad, and oversized pig. Rani knew everything about Aubrey's life, since she would tell it to anyone within earshot at any given moment.

What she didn't know was how fast news of the computer lab incident had travelled. She didn't know how fast it would get to Aubrey, all the way back in the sixth grade.

"Daddy!" called Aubrey in her fake angel voice. Rani recognized it and tensed up immediately, closing her mother's laptop.

"I heard at school today that there was a power outage in just one room!" she said sweetly. "Rani's room."

Rani heard Gavin grumble under his breath before shouting her name. She got off her bed and stood in the doorway.

"Yes?" she asked, as innocently as possible.

"How many times have I told you!" he screamed.

"Freak!"

Rani closed her eyes and tried to tune him out.

"I open my doors to you and your mother and what do I get!" he roared. "A nutcase! It's just not right, putting Christian children with you, you little demon!" the shouting continued, but Rani tuned it out. Her mind was far away. Her mind was in a place safe from everyone who didn't understand, with people who would get her, and be like her. She was with the other strange occurrences.

Later that evening, her mom went into her room. Rani was sitting on the bed, the laptop open onto an article about a school bus saved under mysterious circumstances by an unknown child who later vanished.

Rani's mother was a short woman, with thin, curly brown hair and ditch-water brown eyes. Rani remembered when her mom had been beautiful. It had been before her dad had walked out. Her mom had been broken since that day. Rani didn't remember much, of course, she had fallen down the stairs the day before, and had sustained memory loss from a concussion.

Her mother walked over to the bed, pausing at the ladder that she would have to climb to get onto the top bunk. Rani ignored her, reading further into the article.

"Sweetheart," Rani's mother cooed, but Rani stared at the article, tears burning in her eyes. "I'm sorry Gavin shouted at you. What happened?" Her mother asked. She sounded tired, as if it had worn on her too much already.

"Same as every time," Rani said bitterly. "I lost my temper." She slammed the computer shut, wincing as the lights flickered. When Gavin did not yell at her from the TV room, bedroom, bathroom, or the pub downtown, she relaxed.

"You have to try to keep it in, Rani," her mother pleaded.

"I can't live like this forever!" Rani spat, glaring at her mom. The lights flickered once again, and Rani's eyes widened in terror. She heard a shout from Ethan, one of the twin step monsters Gavin had brought with him, but other than that silence. Rani lowered her voice, hissing, "I can't always keep it in, and it's just getting worse."

Rani's mother groaned, rubbing her fingers against her temples. She looked tired, and Rani felt bad. She had lost a lot; a daughter and a husband. Rani didn't let it show, instead keeping her face twisted with venom.

"Please try ," Her mother begged. "Please."

Rani turned to the computer, which she opened back up. She bit her lip. "I'll try ," she whispered as her mom walked out of the room.

It was over a week later. The girls hadn't bugged her since then, but she had heard the whispers. They called her a freak, just like Gavin, Aubrey, her mom, everyone.

Everyone but her dad. He had been the only one who had understood her.

She sat in some class that she hadn't paid attention to in weeks. She twirled the lightning bolt in her fingers. She was waiting. Waiting for a moment that drags her from this prison of a life she had been condemned to. Her whole world was like a prison. Something inside her told her that she'd never be free, but she fought that thought with every inch of her being. Everything she was, had been, or ever would be depended on her getting out of this prison.

She gazed out the window at the cool fall breeze blowing the leaves around. Rani sighed. She looked around the room. A cross dangled from a few girls necks. In fact, as she gazed around more, she noticed that everyone had a cross on. Some had it written on their hands, some on rings or necklaces. She caught someone's eye, and they started fingering nervously with their cross necklace. She turned to the front of the room. She noticed a pretty girl was at the front of the room, saying something. It was one of the girls from the computer lab, a rich girl who felt comletly entitled to everything. Rani rolled her eyes, but she listened. It must have been English, because the girl was reading from a story. Rani quickly realized she had written it. her gut twisted as she listened.

"Bad stuff had happened at the school. Bad, unnatural stuff. There were demons in that school, devils in disguise. It was up to the students to rid the devils from the school. They fought back peacefully, with symbols, and warnings.

They fought back with the one thing that could kill devils." The girl held up her cross necklace around her neck, and smiled, looking right into Rani's eyes. Rani felt shivers travel over her spine, and anger bristle beneath that.

"Lovely story, but really, don't you know that school is no place for religious-"

"It isn't religious, Mrs., this is a narrative. This actually happened." The girl protested. Rani felt her ears burn as the gazes fell on her.

"This is still happening. We are still fighting those devils." the girl said. *Breath,* thought Rani. *Stay calm. Stay calm.*

"What do you mean, this is going on," said her teacher sharply. Rani felt her stomach clench up. *Is that what they thought of her? Did they think she was a devil?*

"There is a devil among is, in this very room even. She sits among students like she normal, but she's not, and-" started the girl, but the teacher cut her off.

"Do you really expect me to believe that?" said the teacher angrily. All eyes were still on Rani. She clenched her desk, trying not to let anger rise. She tried counting to ten softly. She was at six when someone whispered in her ear.

"In Salem, they burn witches. Shame this isn't Salem."

The light bulbs exploded overhead, sending a shower of glass down at the class. Screams sounded. Scratches were all over the arms and face of the class. Darkness spread over the city like a shadow falling over. Rani was the only one scratch free one. The student who was reading the paper looked terrified, clutching the cross like it was a lifeline. A gash spread from the girls temple to the top of her cheek. Rani felt sick was blood oozed out. Everyone in the class was engrossed in getting the glass out of their faces and arms, but the ones that weren't were staring at her. She stood up and ran from the room, eyes burning.

The school was evacuated for "dangerous electrical Surges".

The bus ride home was silent, and the longest bus ride of Rani's life. She what would happen when she got home. People stared at her as if she had three heads. Rani just wanted to cry. She skipped the elevator, taking the stairs, stalling. All too soon, she was at her door. She gulped and walked inside. Gavin's fist collided with her jaw. She recoiled as he boxed her ear. She rubbed her sore jaw. He was heavily drunk, and she could smell alcohol on his breath.

"GET OUT!" he roared, slurring heavily. "Don't you dare show your face in this house ever again!" Tears ran down Rani's face. She ran to her room, narrowly avoiding another blow from Gavin. Her twin step brothers ran from her as they saw her. Aubrey darted from her room. Rani got changed into Aubrey's clothes, dark skinny jeans and a white t-shirt. She pulled on a brown leather jacket, also Aubrey's. As long as she was leaving, might as well. She grabbed a gray back pack and stuffed a blanket and pillow inside. She grabbed anything she cared about and tossed it the bag; a picture frame of her and her dad, her mom's laptop and charger, anything. She pulled a black beanie on to cover her head and worn black gloves over her shaking hands.

She jammed a pair of converse on her feet, and ran back through the living room. Gavin roared and lunged at her, but she was too quick. Rani grabbed the emergency twenty from on top of the fridge and then right out the door. She sped down the stairs, into the lobby, and out onto the parking lot.

It was early afternoon, but the lights of the city were out. Cars were backed up in the streets. The traffic lights were out, and policemen were attempting to direct traffic. The towering buildings were dark, and the whole city looked as if it were shutting down. People had begun to abandon their cars, and the sidewalks were crowded and completely filled. The sky was gray, and the air was brisk, with a little breeze that made the air seem several degrees cooler. Brown leaves blew gently across the street, and they were crushed underfoot by the passersby.

Tears didn't fill her eyes, this had happened loads of times. She walked the streets, picking her way through the crowds and ducked into a store. She stayed there for several hours, pretending to look through the endless racks of clothing. She left when it closed at 8 o'clock. She ate cheaply off the dollar menu of McDonalds, choking down a greasy cheeseburger. She wanted to stay in there as long as she could, inside, safe and warm, and off the streets, but she didn't. She walked out on the streets, waiting until the comforting glow of the streetlights. Rani sat on a park bench, shivering slightly from the cold. She knew that tomorrow her mom would find her and they would leave the city, and start over again, for the third time. She closed her eyes and tried to get some sleep. Right before unconsciousness swept over her, she heard a train whistle as it pulled into the station. Raindrops began falling, washing the tear stains from her face. She sat up.

"Are you kidding me?" she said aloud to no one in particular. "Really?" fat, warm tears ran down her face. She stood up off the bench and grabbed her bag. She ran through the rain towards the brick building that the rushing train was pulling into.

The building was all brick, with concrete flooring. The old station had been converted to a storage facility for a grocery store company, E & T, and so cardboard boxes were stacked all over the place. E & T must have been the only company to still use trains in the entire city. But Rani could hardly complain. She now had a safe dry place to spend the night, since some foolish worker had left the door open. She slipped inside, and crouched behind some boxes.

Rani sat in the station, out of the heavy rain. She watched as the old train pulled through. She watched the workmen unpack box after box from her hiding place near a pile of old discarded boxes.   She had almost nodded off again when she heard a shout. A worker was holding two kids, Rani's age or just older, by the arms.

"Found them hiding in one of the cargo cars," called a gruff worker.

Rani took in them. From where she was sitting, she could just make them out. One was a boy, tall, with broad shoulders. He had surfer blonde style hair, with light freckles across his nose, so light that she could barely tell they were there. His eyes were forest green, and full of mischief.

The other was a girl, looking to be Indian. Her skin was light brown, and she had long dark brown hair. She was skinny, and frail-looking. She had pretty gray eyes. Unlike the boy, she didn't look amused that she was caught.

"What do you think we should do with them?" asked another worker.

The girl looked right into the eyes of the man who was holding her. "Let us go."

His face went slightly slack, and his face gaze a blank expression. His grip loosened on her arm, and she tried to wiggle free. "We should let them go," he said, his voice blank and emotionless.

"Harry, what's wrong with you?" asked another worker, slapping him on the arm. The girl lost eye contact, and the man snapped out of, squeezing her arm again. The girl looked around wildly, panicking. Her eyes rested on Rani for a split second, and in that second, she mouthed help.

Rani was overcome by the gaze for a moment. For a moment, while the girl had eye contact with her, it had been as if someone else was in control of her.

The boy was staring at the door. Rani followed his gaze and started to stand. The rain outside had begun to pour so hard that the streets were flooding.

"Come on, let's go" said the gruff worker. "We're bringing you to the police." The workers holding them started dragging them along. Suddenly, the glass doors leading outside shattered, and a five foot wave off water flooded the group. The workers and the girl were in a puddle on the floor, while the boy stood a grin on his face. He helped the girl to her feet, and they took off, but were stopped by some workers.

Rani ran. She sprinted towards them, her wet hair flying behind her. She got to the group before the workers closed in on them. She dropped her bag in the puddle of water at their feet.

"Get behind me," she said. They obeyed. The workers were several feet in front of them, and Rani stood in front of the girl and boy. *As long as she was leaving the city*, she thought, *might as well.*

She gathered her anger towards Gavin, the kids at her school, Aubrey, everything, let it boil over. Closing her eyes, she threw that energy into the building, and it responded well.

She threw her arms into the air at either side of her. Every bulb in the place burst into flame before shattering, throwing the glass at the workers. They shielded their faces, and their clothes took most of the blow.

She turned and looked at the group behind her, expecting to see them terrified of her. Instead, the boy was grinning, and the girl had a shy sort of smile across her face. Rani was shocked. Normally, people would have screamed, or run, or called her the devil, but they just smiled knowingly.

"How would you like to have an adventure?" said the boy, smiling.

Leaving Home

And so, the next day, Rani was sitting on a train. The boy was sitting by some boxes, his head to his chest, sleeping. Rani sat next to the girl.

"My name's Lydia," she said.

"I'm Rani. Rani McSean"

They rode in silence for a while. Rani had never really tried to make friends since her dad died. What did she even say?

"So, do you guys ride trains illegally often?" said Rani. *Crap,* she thought. *That sounded a lot better in my head than out loud.* Lydia laughed. *Good,* Rani thought. *She thinks I'm joking and not just socially awkward.*

"Well," Lydia started, "I'm from New York. I ran away because my Mom and Dad were scared of the stuff I could do. I took a train, legally, to Chicago, which is where I meet Garret." She motioned to the boy. "He told me about a place he had heard about up in Michigan. A place that's safe for kids like us. We've been riding trains illegally to get there for two weeks. Most of the time we only go about fifty miles before we are discovered."

"Oh," said Rani.

Train hit a bump, and Garret fell forward. He leapt to his feet, grabbing something from his bag. He held it out in front of him, and Rani realized it was a sword. She scooted back.

"Trailers, mutants, or Superiors?" he asked wildly.

"Neither," said Lydia. "A bump in the track." Garret stuffed the sword back into his bag.

"Question," said Rani, "why does he have a sword?"

"It's for when we are attacked." Lydia said simply.

"Follow-up question, when are we going to be attacked?" asked Rani.

"Well, the trailers are government agents in charge of making people like us disappear, but we can't hurt them, only hide. Superiors are people with these… differences… who think they are better than everyone. Anyone who doesn't agree, they attack. We can hurt them," said Garret.

"What about Mutants?" asked Rani, still confused.

"Mutants are people who got a bad dose of whatever made us like this," said Lydia. "They normally don't look human, but you really never know. They have mental disabilities that cause them to be bloodthirsty. 75% of people in jail are mutants, but humans can't see their true form."

"Humans?" asked Rani. "Last I checked, I was a human."

"Not technically." Said Lydia. "These abilities make us

belong to another species. One mutated virus, from radiation in the 20's, and boom! Three human breeds: average, everyday humans; us, otherwise known as Clessi; and then the really unlucky ones, the Mutants."

Rani's head was spinning. "Why can't humans tell the Mutants from normal people?"

"A part of the brain, the one that separates reality from dreams and imagination, it translates the look of them into what the humans want to see, expect to see, instead of what they are seeing. We don't have that part of the brain. It lies dormant. Instead, we have a different part of the brain awakened, and that is what gives us these abilities," said Lydia. Seeing Rani's confused face, she added, "its science, not magic."

Rani nodded. "That sword," Lydia said, "is made of Carndium, an element that humans can't see. It doesn't exist in their reality. It also can't hurt them. Mutants, and us, however, it hurts us quite well. "

Garret sat down beside Rani. "Mutants can smell powerful Clessi. They will be after us soon. We have run into three so far, and that was just two of us. You've got a lot of power, judging from what you did last night."

Lydia nodded. "What exactly was that?" she asked. "I've never read about anyone being able to do that before."

"I control electricity" said Rani.

"Can you control lightning?" asked Garret, his eyes wide.

"Duh, Garret, lightning is a form of electricity," said Lydia. "Please excuse him, he's rather stupid. He is mostly brawn, and very little brain."

"Hey!" exclaimed Garret. "Just because I'm not a know-it-all doesn't mean I'm stupid!"

"What's the capital of New Hampshire?" asked Lydia smugly.

"That's not fair!" Garret said angrily. "Ask me stuff that actually matters!"

Rani ignored their useless bickering and looked down at her hands. She wondered if she could control lightning. She had never tried it before, which was probably good, since she would probably have killed someone, most likely herself.

She could feel the train slowing down, and Garret and Lydia must have too, because they grabbed their bags and stopped arguing. The train stopped, and they trio climbed out of the cargo car they had hidden in and out into the midmorning sun.

It was cool, being late fall, and the leaves were blowing off the trees and gently floating in the wind. They were in a small town, old buildings dominating most of the downtown that they had pulled into. Rani rubbed the lightning bolt and locket between her fingers nervously as she glanced around the town. On their side of the road, forest lined the road, and then there were railroad tracks and the brick station. The woods were a mass of orange, yellows and reds, with leaves blanketing the ground. Leaves blew gently in groups around their feet and onto the road.

"Where are we?" Rani questioned.

"Ellicot, a town almost a hundred miles from the Safe Zone," answered Lydia. She pulled her gray wool jacket closer around her shoulders. A chill crept through Rani's leather jacket, sending shivers up her spine.

"The next train leaves toward the safe zone tomorrow," Garret announced, looking at a schedule. "Until then, we'll hang around here."

The group walked towards one of the stores to stay in and away from the wind for a while. They were on their toes, careful and cautious. Rani was over by the candle section, inhaling all the wonderful aroma's when she saw something odd. Across the street, in the woods, something was moving. Something big. For a moment she could have sworn she saw glowing eyes, but she pushed the idea to the back of her mind. It was her imagination playing tricks on her. She had been nervous ever since Garret and Lydia had told her about the Mutants. It was probably nothing. She picked up another candle and smelled it. *Yes,* she thought, *it was defiantly all in my head.*

Lydia was in the book section of the store, sitting cross

legged, a novel in her lap. She thumbed through the pages quickly, nearly three times as fast as any normal person would have. Her mind was incredibly disciplined to absorb the information as fast as she could, and a stack of books was beside her, ready to be started.

Garret wandered the store, uneasily. Something was off about this place. The energy was all wrong. He let out a shudder, even though the temperature of the store was well above the temperature outside. He gripped the handle of his sword without taking it from his backpack. Something was very wrong. He paced up and down the aisle quickly, attracting weird looks from the other customers in the store.

Rani was admiring another set of candles. She had never smelled anything so wonderful in her life as these candles. They sure smelled a lot better than the nasty apartment back home. She felt a pang of guilt. Her mom must be worried sick right now. She would have to send a call and tell her where she was. Maybe the town had a post office...

A movement to the right caught her eye, and she turned toward the road once again. Something in the woods was moving again, shifting branches and leaves out of the way. Rani walked up to the window and peeked through. More movement shook through the branches. Rani pressed her face up against the window, peering at the woods on the other side. She saw a big, dark shadow looming in the woods. The glowing eyes focused on her.

Rani stumbled back, nearly knocking over a display shelf. "Garret!" she called. "Lydia!" She ran through the store. "Garret!" she panted. "Lydia!" She ran through the store, knocking over displays as she ran. She grabbed the back of Lydia's coat and pulled her to her feet.

"We've got a problem," she panted. Lydia looked at her and paled.

"What happened?" she asked. Her face turned towards Garret, who was racing at her.

"Take a good look outside," he said. They rushed to the front of the store, where through the window, a mutant could be seen on the street. It stood on two feet, and looked like a tall man, except it's clothes were torn, and its skin was green. Its eyes glowed Yellowish, and it had a mouth full of black razor sharp teeth, jagged like bits of pointed glass. Large purple and blue veins could be seen on its head, which was completely bald. It looked at them and roared, spit flying.

Rani gulped. "I should have stayed home," she cried.

Garret drew his sword. His face was all business.

"Let's get him," he said, his face set like stone. He dropped his bag at the girls' feet and ran out onto the street.

"Are you insane?" yelled Rani, but he was already gone.

"This happens all the time," Lydia assured her.

"Where did he get that sword?" asked Rani

"His father is also a Clessi."

Rani turned to look at the street, and watched as Garret ran at the Mutant.

"Should we be helping?" asked Rani. Lydia gave her a sideways glance.

"Do you want to be killed?" She asked. Rani sighed. She dropped her bag at her feet and walked out the door. The Mutant was just throwing Garret against a brick wall. He hit hard and slumped to the ground. Rani ran over to him and knelt beside him. He shook his head and climbed to his feet. Rani stood beside him. She raised her hands in fists, in an awkward fighting stance. Garret raised his sword.

"Get back inside," he muttered.

"Not on your life!" Rani yelled as she gathered her feelings. She needed to get angry. She could feel the hums of the electrical wires above her, and she focused on it. She marveled at how calm the town was. How was no one noticing this?

As hard as Rani was focusing, nothing was happening. No light bulbs were shattering, the street lights remained intact, and no power lines were going willy-nilly. Garret was slicing wildly at the Mutant, who was waving its huge fists around. Blood gushed from several wounds on the chest and arms of the Mutant. Garret flung his sword at the green monster. It hit it in the chest, and it stumbled and fell forward. The electricity fizzled off of Rani as the Mutant hit the ground. Garret ran forward and finished off the beast.

Lydia ran over to Garret. "Are you alright?" she asked. Rani stopped trying to gather electricity. She ran over to Garret. His nose was bleeding, and Lydia reached into her bag and grabbed a handful of fast food napkins. He held them to his nose and shoved his sword into his bag.

"What were you thinking," he spat at Rani. "You could have gotten killed!"

"I didn't!" she exclaimed.

"Don't ever pull anything like that again." He said, turning away. Rani blew the hair out of her eyes, angry. Sparks crackled in her clenched hands. She breathed heavily, and shook out her hands, shooting the sparks harmlessly out into the air. Why could she conjure electricity now, and not when she had needed it? She breathed deeply, letting out her anger. She watched as the monster dissolved into a massive puddle of green goo. Rain started pouring down, sweeping the goo into the sewer drains. Surprisingly enough, the people seemed to notice the rain more than they did the fight. They pulled out umbrellas and ran into stores. Lydia gave Rani and Garret their bag, and the trio walked towards a fast food joint down the road.

"You didn't tell me they dissolved." Rani said.

"Sometimes they do, sometimes they don't," answered Lydia. They trudged into the restaurant, soaking wet. Rani ordered them food with the leftover money. They sat in booth, Garret nursing his nose, and Lydia scanning the outside for any other Mutants.   Rani sat between them, practically spitting mad. She had only tried to help, and Garret had treated her like crap. She was furious, but her anger slowly dissolved as she watched Garret shove the third napkin up his nose. How could she be mad at someone who was injured? She would be mad at him when his nose stopped bleeding. She handed him another napkin as he tilted his head back.

"You're supposed to tilt your head forward when you have a nosebleed," said Lydia, and Garret rolled his eyes.

"Thidia, stawp behing tho annoyting," he said, pinching his nose shut. Rani laughed, and Lydia smiled.

"Thwats tho thunny?" He said. Lydia started laughing now, and Rani covered her mouth with her hands. "Thits thot thunny!"

"You're right," said Rani, her face serious. "Thits thiliarious."

She and Lydia started laughing again, and Garret gave in, and his mischievous smile took over his face.

"Anyone want seconds?" asked Rani, holding out the remaining five dollars. They shook their heads, and they headed out of the store. It was still raining, and they ran to the next place. It was a book store, and Lydia looked as if she had died and gone to heaven.

Garret and Rani sat in some comfy old chairs, Garret with napkins hanging out of his nose. His goofy grin was back, and Rani felt better. She couldn't stay mad at him. He was pretending to be reading so the owner, an elderly man, wouldn't through them out. He held an old novel upside down, while whispering to her.

"What made you run away?" He asked, and Rani sighed. She told him everything. About Gavin, Aubrey her mom, the kids at school, but before all of that, she told him about her dad. She told him about the necklace, and the car accident that had changed her life forever.

"What's your story?" asked Rani, a smile curling her lips as he turned a page in the upside book.

"I lived in a city. My dad is Clessi, and so is my brother, Andrew. They're jerks, both of them. Dad's always experimenting, pushing the limits of what he can do. He ruined my little sister with one of these experiments. He injected Mutant blood into my mom's food when she was pregnant. When my sister was born, She was a third of everything." He took a folded up photo out of his pocket. It showed him, a tired-looking blonde lady who must have been his mom, and a small girl. The girl had a frightened look on her face. One wide eye was green, like Garret and his mom's, and the other was yellow, like a hawks. Her mouth was slightly ajar, and Rani could see that the girl had fang-like teeth. Her skin was pale, with a grayish tint to it. She held her mom's hand tightly, and Rani saw the iron grip had left bruises on the mom's both hands. The girl had a faraway look in both eyes.

"She has a split personality. Her human part mixes with the Mutant blood like poison, and it will kill her by the time she's twelve," he pointed to the blackish-blue veins on the girls neck. "Her Mutant side causes her to lash out against me and my brother. My dad wants her as a weapon, but my mom loves her more than anything in the world, even though she is like a demon when she loses control of her Mutant side. Her human and Clessi side are angelic, though." He tucked the photo back into his pocket. "my dad tried to recruit me to go with him, and Andrew, and do stuff like that. He doesn't know I'm gone yet. He won't know for a few weeks. He's never home, and my mom wanted me to be as far away from him as possible."

Rani nodded. Compared to him, her life sounded like a walk in the park. She looked back at her own book and turned the page to make it look like she was reading. She looked back over at Garret, and noticed for the first time the scars on the side of his neck. Thin white lines, almost faded now, but not quite.

Rani looked over to Lydia, through the rows of books. She sat cross-legged on the floor, her nose deep in a book. The pages turned quickly, and Rani had never seen anyone so focused before.

"What would you do to be normal?" Rani asked Garret.

"Why would you ever want to be normal? Some people spend their whole lives trying to be something unique. I would hate to just be another human in a boring human world. I want to stick out. I want to be remembered."

"I just want to fit in somewhere," Rani said, leaning back in her chair.

"Don't try to fit in. try to stand out." said Garret. He got up, and set down the books. Rani set down her book.

He pulled their backpacks over next to Lydia, who didn't even look up to acknowledge his existence. Then he waked back over and grabbed Rani's hand. He pulled her off the chair and onto her feet.

"Come on," he said, pulling her behind him. She followed him out of the store, and onto the street, where the rain was still pouring down. When they were outside, Rani saw that Garret had taken off his sweatshirt. He still held her hand, and Rani felt her cheeks glow red. He led her out into the middle of the street.

"What are we doing?" Questioned Rani, looking around. No cars were on the road, but people were watching from windows of stores and sidewalks. Rani looked back and forth at them, avoiding eye contact. "Garret, people are staring. What are we doing?"

"Standing out." He stated, letting go of her hand. "May I have this dance?"

Rani laughed, but Garret placed on hand on her waist, and the other in hers. He grinned before they started dancing.

The people from the shop windows watched as for the next two hours, a pair of teenagers that no one had ever seen before danced around to music only they could hear, surrounded by the crystal drops of rain falling around then. The rain seemed to lighten around them, becoming slower, and more beautiful, but no one thought much of it, except for the pair.

Rani looked around her as she danced, amazed at the slow falling drops of rain all around her. They were ornate, like diamonds falling from the sky, shimmering iridescent colors as they sprinkled down around them. Garret looked into Rani's big, blue eyes, and wide smile, and thought that he had never seen anyone so caught in a moment so perfectly, so beautifully, in his life. In that moment, something changed between them, something clicked, and they both felt it. They had gone from strangers to friends in two days, and Rani didn't want to be without these two people ever again, because she had felt loneliness, and now she had felt a taste of a piece of heaven on earth called friendship.

When they went back inside the book shop, soaked to the bone, Lydia looked up from her book at their wide smiles.

"What happened to you?" She asked, gasping at the sight of them all wet. She pulled the stack of books away from them, protecting them from the drips of water that was pooling into puddles at their feet. Rani pulled of her soaked leather jacket and set it down on the floor by her bag. The white t-shirt underneath clung to her like a second skin. Lydia scooped up two books in her arms, piling the rest on a nearby shelf.

"Come on," She moaned, picking up her backpack. "The manager has been evil eyeing you two since we got back in here." She walked over to the old man behind the counter, and Rani grabbed her backpack and her jacket. Garret picked up his bag as well and swung it over his shoulder. Rani could see the sword glint out of it, and shivered. Balled up napkins were still shoved up Garrets nose, and blood was spattered across the top of his shirt.

"We are going to have to get you a new shirt," Rani decided, and Garret looked down, his cheeks so red that the light brown freckles vanished. Lydia walked back over to them, the books in a plastic bag so they couldn't get wet. She tucked the bag inside of her backpack, along with something clutched in her other hand.

"What's that?" asked Rani.

"What's what?" asked Lydia, her voice too light and carefree.

"Lydia, what is that?"

"I don't know what you're talking about."

Rani reached into Lydia's backpack, pulling out two ten-dollar bills.

"Where did you get these?" Rani had to say it twice before Lydia answered.

"I'm sorry, I can't always help it," She began mumbling, and Rani couldn't understand her anymore.

"Can't always help what?" questioned Rani.

"The man paid me to buy the books. I accidently used my ability on him." Lydia cried, her face guilty and upset. "I didn't mean to, but I was looking in his eyes, and I thought about how nice it would be to have some money that we could spend, and he just gave it to me because I was thinking about it. He didn't even charge for the books!" She hung her head, staring at the floor.

"Lydia, its fine. I really just wanted to know, ok?" Rani assured her.

"You don't think it's weird?"

"Of course not!" Rani exclaimed. "I exploded some light bulbs and you didn't think it was weird!"

Lydia smiled at her, and Rani smiled back.

They left the store, heading to the next one. It was a

consignment shop, and there they bought Garret a shirt that didn't have blood on it. It was a blue shirt that had some college logo on it that none of them recognized. Rani bought a thick gray sweater, since it would be winter soon, and she would need something to wear. Lydia went straight to the used supply section and searched through the books until she found one she liked. All together, they only spent ten dollars.

They drifted store to store throughout the afternoon, keeping arm and dry. At nightfall, when the last store on the small main street had closed, the group sat in the bottom of the playground equipment in the town's park. They were underneath the play castle, where the fake dungeon was. The ground was sand, and it was not yet soaked.

It was dry down there, and after gathering sticks from nearby trees, Rani used sparks to create the smallest bonfire in the world. They spread out blankets and lay down around it, using it more as light than warmth.

The group was eating from a can of spaghetti-o's that Lydia had gotten using her abilities at one of the stores. She had gotten three, and they had already eaten one, pledging to save the rest for an emergency. They could only heat one can up at a time using Rani's mini fire, and they passed it around in a circle, each using their own plastic spoon. Rani had out her mother's laptop, and was using the town's post office's Wi-Fi to surf the web.

She searched out her name, and saw the news report. She had been reported as a run away. Her mom and Gavin were reported as franticly looking for her. Aubrey had been interviewed about it, making sure to add that they shared a room, and that she had taken her clothes.

"Little brat," Rani murmured as she scrolled through the interview.

"What?" asked Garret, his mouth full of food.

"My little step sister is becoming quite an attention hog over me going missing. Like she misses me," Rani snorted.

"I wonder if my family misses me." Lydia said, closing up her book.

"Let's find out," announced Rani, clicking the search bar. "What's your last name?"

"Niles." She said, "Lydia Niles."

Rani typed it in the search domain, and news reports popped up.

"Lydia Niles of New York City," Rani Read, "was reported to have run away on Thursday. It was yet another tragic blow against the family, whose oldest son, Henry, had run away two years before had. Her mom, dad, three brothers and one sister grieve for their missing daughter, praying that she will come home safe and sound."

Lydia nodded. "Henry was a Clessi too," she said to them. "He would be seventeen if he did make it to the Safe Zone.

"What about you, Garret?" asked Lydia. Rani and Garret exchanged glances.

"My mom knows I ran away. Encouraged it, in fact. My dad doesn't know, so she won't let the news out until days before he swings by home, so that he can't come look for me before I make it safely."

Lydia nodded, her expression grave. "That's tough," she said. Rani passed her the can, and Lydia finished it up.

"We should probably get some sleep," Lydia pointed out, "but someone will have to stay awake and watch out for attackers." She had barely finished the sentence when she yawned loudly.

"I'll take the first watch," Garret volunteered, and Lydia took off her little silver watch and handed it to him. "Wake the next person around midnight."

"I'll go second," Rani stated before lying down fully. She crawled under her blanket, lying on top of the cold sand. Her jacket was still wet, along with her white t-shirt, and she had hung them both to dry nearby. She wore only her jeans and her sweater, and shivered. She closed her eyes and drifted off into sleep almost instantly, wrapping herself in the thick blanket of unconsciousness.

SARAH ELIZABETH

The Ugly Truth

Mrs. Heft sat at the kitchen table, sobbing. Her shoulders shook as the former Mrs. McSean cried over the second daughter of hers to run away. She stared at the picture frame that held Robert McSean, smiling at the camera.

Robert McSean was a tall man, with messy brown hair and cobalt blue eyes. His face was covered in a thin layer of stubble, and he was standing with his arm around Rani. She was a spitting image of her father; the same eyes and long legs struck the family resemblance well.

The picture was taken a month before his mysterious drowning.

"Why me?" she asked. "Why did my daughters have to get dragged into this?"

The picture frame did not respond. Mrs. Heft pulled her wedding ring to Gavin Heft off her finger and threw it across the room, embedding it in the wall. She slammed her hands down angrily, cracking the table. All these years, and she never had the control over her powers. Robert had. He had been able to bend al his powers to his will as easily as writing his name. It had been easier with him here.

Jessamine Heft had been expecting to tell her two daughters with her late husband about the Clessi. She had wanted to help them to the Safe Zone. She had wanted to move to a town just outside of it, be able to visit. She had always known, somehow, that that wouldn't work. From the second she had laid eyes on her second daughter, she knew there was power there, the likes of which she had never seen before. The lights had flickered while she was in labor. They had exploded when the baby was born. Rani had shorted out their first house at sixteen months.

When Rani had caused a power outage her first day of kindergarten, Robert had been there to fix the damage. When her firstborn daughter had had the first signs of her power, he alone had calmed her down.

Robert had been there when Jessamine had thrown a chair through the wall of their house after Sylvia ran away. He had helped Rani hid her ability. They had put off telling her for years. And now Rani McSean was out there, unaware of her parents abilities.

Jessamine hadn't used her powers since the day she had watched her husband, her Robert, taken from their house. The last words she ever heard were off him telling them that he was the only one in the house. He was the only freak. He screamed to leave the rest of them.

Rani was locked in a closet, sobbing. Jessamine had held her terrified child, praying that they wouldn't be found. The dogs had, of course. The famous beasts of the Superiors had sniffed them out. Jessamine had put up a fight. Rani was thrown against a wall. A concussion was just the cover up Jessamine had needed to convince Rani it was a dream, and that her father had walked out on them.

A month later, when the body of Robert McSean had washed up on the shore of a lake a few hours from there, Jessamine had told her daughter the lies the police had settled with. It was a suicide. Robert McSean, the bravest, strongest, most caring man Jessamine had ever known, was remembered as committing suicide, and not for what had actually happened.

As Jessamine knew all too well, sometimes it was better to let them believe the lies rather than tell them a truth. The truth had never gotten her anything but heartache. The truth had made her first daughter, her little girl, run as far away as she could. Her second daughter had followed without the truth. Was there any right choice to have made?

Could anyone really blame her for hiding such a secret?

Could Rani ever forgive her for hiding such a secret?

Leaving

The air was crisp with the scent of rotting leaves and cool air, the smell of fall. A gentle breeze sent chills up the spines of passerby's, and the trees were stripped bare of all leaves, left with nothing to hide.

Rani slept until almost noon the next day. When she woke up, the train was still not there. The fire was a pile of embers and ash, and Garret was burying it under the sand. Lydia was reading, and sat on top of the sand, oblivious to everything but the book.

Rani sat up, shocked.

"Why didn't you wake me?" she said, annoyed.

"You were so tired, and I really lost track of time," he explained, but Rani still looked irritated. "Honestly!" he said, crossing his heart with his right hand. Rani sighed and threw the blanket off of her. It was light out, but the sunlight barely peeked its bright head into the shaded crevice they had invaded for the night. Cold engulfed Rani in a matter of seconds, and she shivered. She noticed a second blanket was in with hers.

"You were shivering when you went to sleep," Garret shrugged, giving her a sideways smile. Rani smiled back at him and folded up both blankets, handing Garret his. She found it was impossible to stay mad at him for anything, since he keep surprising her with nice things he did. *Geez*, Rani thought, *he is making it impossible to be mad at him over him not letting her help with the fight.*

Rani's thoughts were interrupted by the loud train whistle as they heard it chug into the station. Lydia looked up from her book.

"Train's here," Lydia announced.

"Very good, Lydia!" Garret announced. "You're so smart!"

Lydia shot him a death stare, but Rani giggled as she packed away the clothes she had set out to dry. They were still a bit damp, but Rani packed them in with her bag anyway. They walked to the station, trying to act as casual as possible before breaking into one of the cars.

The train was old, red with rust, and covered in graffiti. It was cold inside, since it was all metal, but it was safe. They all sat down on boxes, and Garret took a deck of cards from his bag. Rani snapped her fingers, and the lights of the car snapped to life.

Garret shuffled the cards in his hands. "Want in?"

"Sure," said Rani, sitting down on one of the boxes. "Deal."

They played throughout the day, laughing, talking, and just being teenagers. Not kids anymore, but not adults yet. They had all but forgotten the attack of yesterday, but someone had not.

The Superiors watched the train pass from a distance. They knew the children were on it, and they watched with pleasure as the train rumbled by. The train would be stopped, yes, they were sure of that. They had Clessi waiting just outside their silly Safe Zone. The greyhounds at the edge of the leash barked wildly, smelling the young Clessi as the train passed by. The Superior pulled on the leash, silencing the dogs. *They must be powerful,* he thought, *for the dogs to be this riled up. Maybe, maybe I should check this one out myself. The new Clessi Superiors probably couldn't handle them if they were powerful.*

The train sped off through the rolling hills until it disappeared into the horizon. The Superior disappeared down the hill, a long dark coat flapping in the wind behind him.

The Superiors

It was early evening, and the group was eating a jar of peanut butter with a spoon from Garrets bag. They hadn't saved any food from the previous day, and they were starving. They scarfed down the family sized peanut butter jar in less than twenty minutes. Rani had been playing with the lights for nearly an hour, having unscrewed a light bulb and making it turn on and off at will. Lydia laid across several boxes, her nose buried deep in one of the books she had 'borrowed' from the store. Garret had used his sword to open several boxes, and was now using a t-shirt to clean the Mutant blood off of his sword. The train sped through the woods and through small towns without stopping.

The train bumped along, slowing down quickly. The brakes screeched on the metal tracks, and the train slowed to a halt. The train stopped, and the lights flickered.

"Rani?" asked Lydia nervously.

"It's not me. Someone turned the power out," she said, holding out her light bulb, glowing brightly and steadily, in front of her. The light bulbs above her flickered and went out.

The wind whistled around the train, and Garret held his sword out in front of him. Lydia tucked her book in her bag. She gathered   all of the groups stuff and shoved it into the bags. The dogs barking grew closer, and the hairs on the back of Rani's neck stood on end. She could hear the crunch of feet against the gravel that lined the tracks. She held her breath, afraid that in the silence, her breathing could be heard. The dogs' barks were so loud now, Rani was sure they were right in front of them now.

The air must have dropped fifteen degrees in three seconds, because suddenly, they were all shivering. Ice crystals spread slowly across the surface of the metal train car. Their breath began to turn white in the air, and Lydia rubbed her hands together to warm them.

The group watched in wonder as the walls around them froze with a layer of solid ice, leaving the starch walls white and unmarked.

The door creaked open, and light flooded into the train car. Standing outside was a woman, her hair long and white, held back by a thick light blue headband, the same color as her eyes. Her skin was pale, nearly white, and she was dressed in a stylish, but not very warm looking, light blue parka and white scarf. She wore skinny jeans and white boots that were nearly knee high. Her eyes seemed to chill Rani as she looked at her. The other was a man, heavy-set with broad shoulders, and huge fists and black pupils. His crooked smile revealed a mouth full of sharp, jagged teeth.

Rani shivered involuntarily. Were they Clessi or Mutants? The man certainly seemed like a Mutant to her.

Garret stepped in front of the girls, holding his sword out in front of him.

"What do you want?" he asked, trying to sound braver

than he was.

The woman smiled, showing her snow white teeth. "We need you to come with us. We don't mean to hurt you," She said, touching the tip of Garrets sword with a pale finger. Ice crystals spread across the silvery blade, leaving spirals of ice.

"Who are you?" asked Garret, holding his sword more threateningly.

"We are a group of beings who wish to express our dominance over human-" Garret swung the sword at the man, screaming "Superiors!"

The man was taken by surprise, and fell back onto the snow, a large cut across his chest. Rani lunged at the woman, tackling her to the ground. She wrestled with the woman, and Garret struggled to fight off the man while Lydia sat, helplessly watching.

The man launched Garret against the wall, and swung his humungous fists at him. Meanwhile, the woman grabbed Rani's arms. Ice spread across them, making them numb with cold. Rani cried out in pain. She focused, putting her energy into the light bulb which had been thrown aside. It exploded, sending glass into the woman's' legs. The temperature dropped several more degrees, and Rani shivered even more. She ran into the woods, the woman hot on her heels. Rani grabbed a branch from the ground, swung it at the woman, catching her full in the stomach. The woman groaned and then wretched the branch from

Rani's hands. She threw it aside and ran at her. Rain started pouring down, and Rani heard a heavy crash as the man attacking Garret slammed into the train.

The rain around Rani turned hard, and soon, it was hailing all around her. The woman swept her arms in big, arching motions towards her, and the ice balls launched themselves at her. Rani winced as they hit her face and arms. It was like getting hit by golf balls. Rani heard a few more thuds, but she couldn't be sure. She waved her arms wildly, trying to hit away the hail. A few hit her square in the head, and she swayed unevenly. She was cold, hurt and annoyed. As she battled the hail, the woman walked at her. She held what looked like a cross between an icicle and a knife, but Rani wasn't in the mood to find out. She swung at her, slicing a gash on her cheek. Anger burned hotter than pain through Rani. Perfect conditions to try to fight back. She balled her hands in fists, and summoned the energy from the deepest corners of her soul.

Come on, she thought. *Come on! It's now or never!*

Her hands came alive with dancing blue electricity. She swung at the woman, sending a thousand volts into her attacker. It only did enough damage to send the woman stumbling, but it had stopped the worst of the hail. She stumbled dizzily and tripped on her own feet. The ice woman raised the knife that looked eerily like a sharp icicle and trust it down at Rani, who lay on the ground. Right before it hit her, though, Garret sliced the ice in half with his sword, catching the woman with the flat of the blade, sending her stumbling. He sliced at her, cutting a gash across her cheek, the red blood a bright contrast against her pale skin. The woman glared at him. She smiled an evil smile before turning and vanishing into a flurry of snowflakes. disappearing after a few seconds.

Garret helped the woozy Rani to her feet. His blonde hair stuck to his head, in stringy clumps. He had a bruise forming on his forehead, but otherwise, he was grinning away. The large man laid in a crumpled heap on the ground a few feet away, unconscious. Lydia hopped off the train, perfectly fine, shivering slightly from the cold. They began walking, and as they walked, the frost that covered the trees and train became less and less until it disappeared. Lydia was chattering away, but the others were barely listening.

"You know, one thing still is bugging me," she said, a puzzled look on her face. "What ever happened to the dogs?"

Stolen

The second Lydia said that, Garret whipped around, his sword drawn. No one was behind them, but he was still on edge. They formed a tight circle, their backs together. A figure jumped from the top of the train, landing in front of them. Three big Rottweiler's circled in around them from the woods. They snapped at the group's legs, but Garret smacked them with the hilt of his sword.

"Well, well, well," he said, "It would seem that there is one brain between all of you." The figure before them was tall, like a mountain, and a large black trench coat hung below his knees. His black hair was greased against his head, and he stared at them from behind dark eyes.

"Garret, son, how have you been?" he asked, stepping forward to greet him, but Garret held the sword up threateningly.

"You're no father of mine," Garret sneered. Rani gave Garret a sideways glance. Garret shot her an apologetic look. Garret's dad pretended to be wounded, holding his hand over his heart.

"You should be at home with your mother," he said. " I didn't know you had left." Rani clenched her fists, gathering electricity into them. She looked around. There were no light bulbs to be seen. Rain began to pour down hard and heavy. Water began to soak her jeans, and she squirmed uncomfortably.

"Go home, Garret," his father sneered, curling his lip.

Garret ran at his dad, his sword raised, swinging wildly. His father sent the gravel flying at him, knocking him over. Cuts began to bled on Garrets face and arms, and Rani felt her anger manifest. She smacked her hands together, sending electricity at Garret's dad. He stumbled backwards, whacking his head against the train.

Rani grabbed Lydia's hand and pulled her after herself, taking off running. Garret leapt to his feet and started running. The dogs came after them, snapping at their heels, and barking wildly, but the group easily outran them. Fear was the best kind of fuel for running. It didn't stop when it ran out of energy, it stopped when it was out of danger, and for the trio was almost never out of danger.

At any second, a Mutant could jump out of the woods at attack them. The rain slowed to a sprinkle, then finally stopped. Rani's wet hair beat against her back as she ran, sending drops of water flying behind her. The temperature was much warmer here, and she unzipped her jacket, revealing the dry white shirt underneath. The cool fall air was only fifty degrees, but it was a lot warmer than the twenty degrees and hail that had come earlier.

A strange thing happens when you are in true danger. Adrenaline rushes through you. You run faster. You hit harder. You feel stronger. None in the group had ever been as afraid as they were by the Superiors. None of them had ever ran track, but had anyone seen them running, they would have thought at one that they were running machines, fastest of any runner who dared go against them. Being Clessi, they did have a slight advantage. The muscles were stronger. They tired slower. They were simply more evolved.

The group didn't know how far they ran. They had far outrun the stopped train, and into the stretch of woods surrounding the train tracks. The dogs had given up the chase nearly a mile back, and the group was tired, but knew if they stopped, danger would overtake them. Rani's head spun. So far, a Mutant had tried to kill her, along with two Superiors, and Garret's father. For the record, a bunch of dogs had as well, but they weren't half as scary as the ice lady or the Mutant. Finally, a building on the horizon, Lydia collapsed, panting. The other two sat down beside her, gasping for air. Seat poured off their foreheads, and their legs felt like Jell-O, but somehow, they stood up and supported each other as they walked towards the town.

As they got closer, they realized it wasn't a town. The tracks had turned away from the large building, but the group had seen it from there, and had walked through the narrow strip of forest, tripping over every twig and rock on the way. Rani wiped the sweat from her brow. Her breathing had returned to normal, and she had begun toying nervously with her necklaces again. Lydia was breathing like an asthma inflicted patient, but still walked forward slowly, barely keeping up with the other two. Garret was the best off of the two, although cut up and shaken from the encounter with his dad.

They were only two hundred feet from the wall now. Sitting on it was a pretty girl who had to be at least sixteen. She had short blond hair, cut unevenly so that it fell to her shoulders. She had sky blue eyes, and looked at them with an amused expression. She wore skinny jeans, and combat boots. A green military jacket was covering her shirt. A silver dagger was strapped to her leg with tan leather straps. Rani guessed it was Carndium, since no one but a Clessi would probably just be walking around with daggers casually tied to their legs.

The girl stood up, looking incredibly graceful. Rani noticed how powerful she looked. The jeans showed off the bulk muscle in her legs, and the girls arms were tight to the fabric of the jacket, showing of a great deal of muscle. The girl was a fighter, of that Rani was sure.

Lydia had stopped breathing heavily, and was down to just plain old heavy breathing. Rani was realized, since for a while, she had been worried her friend would pass out. Then they would have to carry her, and Rani knew they didn't have the strength to, or the willpower. Most likely, they would have left her here and gone somewhere.

Rani thought back to the Superior attack. That meant that Garrets dad was a Superior. The thought made Rani shudder. No wonder Garret had run away. She had only met Superiors today, and they didn't exactly seem like model parents that would go to school functions and things like that. She had a mental image of Garrets dad sitting in an auditorium full of other parents for a school play. He would probably start running around with his dogs and attack other parents. Rani shivered. Not a fun parent. Not at all like her dad.

Barking filled the air, but the girl was already taking out her dagger. She ran forward, throwing her dagger with deadly accuracy. There was a sharp cry of pain, a loud howl from one nasty dog that was chasing them, before it fell to die. The trio began to sprint, but Rani tripped over a group of rocks. The air was filled with a loud scream, and then sirens filled the air. More people ran up to them. Garret's dad had over taken Rani, who was still on the ground. The blond girl gasped.

"Valen!" She shouted. "Superiors!" People started running from the building, holding weapons. Two girls arrived first.

The first girl was tall, and her light brown hair was braided to the side. She had dark blue eyes, darker even than Rani's. She was skinny, but not wiry like Rani and Lydia, but skinny and strong, with the same incredibly strong body of the blond girl. She wore jeans and a brown wool jacket, belted by a black string of leather that held a knife at her side. She had a bow and a satchel of arrows.

The other girl was short, and slightly pudgy. She had shoulder length wavy red hair pale skin, and freckles, but that isn't what stood out about her most. The thing that most stood out were her ears. They were evenly spaced out on the top of her head, big, sticking right out of her hair. They looked like cat ears, and as the group looked closer, they were. She had large green cat eyes, the pupils like slits in the center. She smiled at them, showing off normal teeth. She held a Carndium dagger.

"Don't worry," She said when she saw the worry in Lydia's eyes. "We'll get your friend back." They rushed into battle against Garret's dad, Valen.

"I'll get them inside" Shouted the blonde girl, taking off. "Follow me!" Lydia and Garret ran after her, fear returning strength to their legs.

"I'm Jaden," said the girl as she ran.

"That is the playing field for normal sports," she said, pointing to the soccer field. " They walked up the massive stone steps to get to the school. Jaden pushed open the large wooden doors, and they entered the building. Guards stood on either side of the doors on the inside. *Mutants must be a big problem*, Lydia thought, tears in her eyes.

"Hey, can you cover my shift for me?" she asked one of the teenaged boys standing guard. "I'm showing them around." The guard nodded and headed outside to take over Jaden's shift, whatever she had been doing sitting out on the wall.

Lydia gasped. The place was huge. It was all stone,

with cloth tapestries on the walls, depicting scenes from fights. Weapons decorated the highest points of the walls, bolted into the stone itself. The ceilings were high, and from the entrance, you could either go up an awe inspiring staircase, or down two corridors to either side. They started walking up the stairs.

"You are probably here because you've been told that you'll be safe and protected. That is not true. You will be responsible for protecting everyone else here, and they will be responsible for protecting you. This is a group of people working together as a unit to stay safe, not a place for scared children. You will be trained, taught how to use your powers, and when you turn 21, you will be sent out into the real world to live as normal of a life as you can get." Jaden said. At the top of the stairs, more guards were posted. Four corridors divided from there, but before that, a stone desk was in the way. A very bored, very old looking man sat at it. His hair was gray and wispy, and his skin was wrinkled like an old shirt. He was shuffling through papers. Jaden walked up to the man.

"I found you two more," she said. "Ones fifteen, ones sixteen," Garrets mouth dropped open. He hadn't told the girl his age!

"Lydia Niles and Garret Valen." The man at the desk looked up.

"Valen?" he asked. Garret shifted uncomfortably.

"I assure you," he said, " I have nothing to do with

the monstrous things my father has done."

" I only knew of the one Valen boy." Said the man, wrinkling his nose in disgust. "The thug Andrew." Garret didn't look all too offended about his brother being insulted. He merely shrugged his shoulders.

"Dad never liked me." He said. "I didn't look like him, and I didn't beat people up like Andrew. I was the black sheep." Jaden looked at him.

"He's telling the truth," she said, and the man nodded. He slid a pair of round reading glasses onto his nose.

"Follow me," she said. "We will go to the girl's room first," she glared at Garret for a moment, then said, "because ladies first, that's why."

Garret was dumbfounded. "I didn't say anything!" he said, shocked.

"She's a telepath, you ninny," said Lydia. Garret smirked. After all that had happened, he was to carefree to even still be concerned that three people had tried killing them today.

They started walking down the second hallway on the right, and Jaden started explaining again. "Girls room in the right two hallways, because girls are always right," they walked past hundreds of wooden doors. "You should get a schedule later tonight about how your days here will go.

You won't get assigned shifts or guard duty until you have been properly trained. Classes are optional, and you can get a high school or college degree while here." Lydia's eyes lit up at the mention of college. "There is a very good chance that there will be people at this school with the same abilities as you. You won't be an outcast here."

They continued down the hallway. Lydia marveled at the fact that weapons still lined the stone near the ceiling. How had they gotten so many weapons? Wasn't it a waste to use them as decoration?

Jaden moved aside and let Lydia in a door. "You be good," she said brightly, closing the door behind her.

The Rescue Team

Lydia had waited all day for news about Rani, but none ever came. She went to classes that day, but her mind was numb with worry. She had waited a long time for a friend, just one friend who understood. Rani had become that friend. Rani had become her best friend. Late that day, Lydia ran into Garret when she was searching for the bathroom. His eyes were red, like he'd been crying. He told her what had happened.

Rani had been taken, along with three others. The two girls they had seen, along with two boys, were sent to chase after them, find where they were hidden, and then report back to the school via phone.

Lydia went from class to class, absorbed in worry. She wasn't thinking about history, or math, or even science; she was thinking about Rani. Days passed like that. Lydia had never had such a problem focusing on her schoolwork before. It had been four days since Rani had gone missing, and Lydia was still in shock.

*   *   *

The group of four trudged on through the thick mud. Katia, the one with fiery red hair and cat ears, hummed softly, more dancing than trudging. The other girl sighed. She was used to her friend being so positive, but this was ridiculous. So far, they had been in a downpour, attacked by five mutants, three superiors, and had to shake a pair of Trailers who had followed them for two whole days.

They climbed up into the back of a flatbed pickup. They knew that the Superiors were heading to Georgia, they had heard it on the first day. Now, the Superiors were far ahead, and they were running late. They hid behind piles of boxes until the man came of the store.

They were in the middle of nowhere, a town with dirt sidewalks, now mud since the downpour, and trees every two feet. The license plate said Florida, which was south from here. They figured they would ride it to Atlanta, Georgia, where the biggest known Superior base was. That must be what they were going with the captives.

Lucas put his arm around her, and the girl, Sylvia, leaned against him. His jacket was still wet from the rain, and his short dark brown hair was soaked, but his mint green eyes smiled down at his beautiful girlfriend. Her brow was furrowed, and the little crease she got when she was nervous about something was across her forehead. She looked up at him, her eyes wide. It had been a long time since he had seen her this sad and worried. It had been six years since he had seen her cry, since her dad had died. She hadn't even cried when she had watched Valen kidnap her friends a few days ago. Heck, she had watched Valen kidnap her little sister and hadn't even shed a single tear.

He looked down into her cobalt blue eyes. "You have done everything you possibly could have done. " When he saw that that hadn't helped, he added, "Your sister will be fine."

"You think so?"

"I know so." He kissed her forehead, and they stayed like that, even after they fell asleep, on the long winding road ahead of them.

Taken

Early in the morning, when the sun was just rising, the stone fortress was wrapped in a thick blanket of fog. The air smelled of decaying leaves and crisp coolness froze the grass, making it crunch under foot. A shrill scream echoed through the stone corridors, bouncing off the high ceilings, sounding into every nook and cranny of the old building. It filled every ear, pulling Clessi from their slumber and out into the halls. The alarm had been raised, and a high siren wail added to the scream. Students ran towards the room where the scream had originated. A large 's' had been painted on the door in dripping red, and once the door was opened, three students were discovered, sobbing at the scene. There was evidence of a struggle that no one had heard in the night. The pillows of one of the beds were shredded, and blood spatters were across the blanket. A student was missing. A girl Clessi, fifteen years old, junior warrior. Students crowded the halls, trying to get a glimpse. Whispers filled the hall, all revolving around the same word. Superiors.

Lydia had woken up with the rest. Being a newbie, she was pushed to the back, finding about what had happened only from whispers.

"Students!" called the man from behind the desk. He stood in front of the door. "A girl has been taken. To insure that this will not happen again, more security parties will be sent out. Lists will be posted outside the door." Moans echoed against the stone walls. Clessi shuffled through the halls, heading back to their rooms.

Lydia got dressed, and headed to battle training. She pulled her hair back into a tight bun, and was about to put on a helmet when the teacher called her name.

"Lydia!" said the trainer harshly. "More students are needed to take on guard and lookout duties. Newbie's cannot do that. You have been advanced to the rank 'trainee warrior'. Report to the Red gym."

Lydia walked through the halls, shaking with excitement. There were four levels of being a warrior, and newbie wasn't one of them. It went Trainee, Apprentice, Junior, and Senior. Once you were in a real level, you could get a real weapon. She got to the Red gym and entered.

No guards were posted at the door, since it was battle training class. The Red gym was large, with red mat floors and stone walls. It was divided into four quadrants, separated by a low stone wall, each specializing in its own weapon.

One was archery, and it faced the wall, with targets hanging on the wall, all different sizes and at different heights. Human sized dummies were spaced along the ground, with Red x's painted where they should hit them. A dozen or so students were at that station.

The next was sword fighting, and it was filled with students in vests and helmets, battling it out. Stone stairs crisscrossed up the wall, and students battled while heading up the stairs, knocking one another off. Large safety nets hung a few feet off the ground below the stairs, but it looked painful to Lydia to fall from fifty feet only to land on a rope net, but it was survivable.

The remaining sections were hand to hand combat and assortment of knives, the kind that Jaden had had strapped to her leg the first day. Targets were set up everywhere in the knife throwing section, and each student was in their own boxed in clear plastic 5x5 area, with moving foam targets of humanoid forms moving at different speeds inside. The hand to hand combat was two students against another two students in a taped in circle much like in the newbie area. A trainer was at each station, yelling orders.

Lydia stood in the doorway until one of the trainers looked up and noticed her. They walked over to her. "You're the new kid, right?" Lydia nodded.

"Let's start you off in archery," they said. "You'll go through every one of these until you find the one that you have the most talent in." They handed her a metal bow with a satchel of arrows and sent her inside the archery center.

"Just shoot until you are out of arrows," they said. "I'll be watching."

Lydia stood in the archery station, shifting uneasily from foot to foot. She wasn't sure about shooting a bow and arrow; she never had before. It had always looked cool in movies to her, but trying it in real life?

She slid the first arrow carefully into the notch and pulled back, surprised at how tense the string was. She aimed at the red x on the head on one of the stuffed humanoid targets. She released the arrow. It flew ten feet before digging into the mat. Discouraged, she notched another and shot it at the same target. It flew past the target and embedded itself into the mat as well. The next few arrows went the same way. She tried a wall target with no luck either. The arrows smashed into stone or into the very edge of the target which didn't count for much. Angry, Lydia bit her lip hard. She shot three more arrows, worse than before. She had one arrow left, nearly no patience, and a sore lip. She took a deep breath and fired. The arrow flew straight and true… into the wall.

"Maybe not archery," said the combat instructor. They walked over to the next section, the knife throwing. She gather a handful of knifes, and entered one of the boxes. She tried to move as fast as the target, but Lydia was not a good shot, missing with every single throw, though doing significant damage to what she did hit, which was mostly the wall and mat. No matter how hard she tried, or how many times she tried, she was a rather terrible aim. She huffed. Fighting was not a skill she could learn from books and classes. It took talent.

The instructor led her over to the sword fighting, handing her a metal sword. It was very plain, and rather boring. Lydia shifted it from hand to hand, getting a feel for its weight.

"Choose your armor," said the trainer, showing her a rack of different kinds of armor. There were shields, heavily plated metal armor, and many more. Lydia chose a thin long sleeve white shirt. It was stiff, and when she inspected it further, she found that it was made of woven steel threads. She put it one, and moved around a bit in it. It became surprisingly fluid once it was on her, barely restricting her movement at all. She lifted her sword, spinning it in her hands.

"Go on," said the instructor. "Your goal is to get up to the top of the staircase and ring the bell. Don't feel discouraged, the kids guarding the stairs are Apprentice level warriors, getting in some extra training."

Even logic didn't make Lydia feel any better about losing to all of them.

*   *   *

Sylvia hated Mutants. She knew it was perfectly normal to, and that it was expected, but she *really* hated them. they had been at a truck stop. A stupid, simple truck stop, and one had run out of the woods and nearly killed her boyfriend.

She fired an arrow into the beast's shoulder. It turned and looked at her. She winced as she saw it. It was short, only two or three feet tall, with large protruding teeth that pushed the lower jaw of the creature back. The skin of it was covered in a dense brown leather-like skin, as if it were a lizard that had gone through one hell of a growth spurt.

Sylvia swallowed hard. Mutants were part human after all, after the 'accident' of tainted water supply in the 20's. *Toxic waste my butt,* she thought as she fired another arrow through the creatures skull. The creature fell with a loud crash, and started shivering as the acidity of its own blood began to eat away at it.

Sylvia pulled Lucas to his feet from where the beast had knocked him. He was shaken, but otherwise alright.

"I'm the Safe Zones top female warrior for a reason," she said when he stared at her in amazement. They climbed back into their ride, and Sylvia was asleep in minutes.

Running Away

Three more students were missing that next morning, with the same grisly scenes as before. Lydia hardly had any time to worry about that, though, and quickly was absorbed by school work completely.

The air outside was cool, and the grass had acquired a thin layer of frost, and footsteps could be heard quite clearly. The brisk fall air fogged up when the warm breath of Clessi students mingled with the cold, numbing air around them. The last of the leaves had fallen, and the bare trees looked naked, with neither a blanket of snow nor leaves to cover up the plain brown bark. It was the clove between seasons, not quite yet to the cold, icy bareness of winter, but not yet out of the brilliant colors and displays of cool, damp fall, with Summer's final 'hurrah' of life clinging on till the bitter, icy end. Checks and noses were rosy from the cold, and hands shook. Gloves, hats, and mittens had become a common sight almost overnight.

Five students had vanished through the night, and Lydia thanked her lucky stars that she wasn't one of them. She only knew a single person who had disappeared, and that helped her keep her calm as she saw the number posted on the main staircase, which had read ten, change to fifteen that day. After lunch was sword fighting in the sword fighting section, pure and simple, without any running, strategies, or drills, simply fighting, and Lydia Hated every second of it. She was a scholar, not a fighter, after all. This was not her thing.

Lydia's heart panged as she realized it had been a week since she had last seen Rani. No word had been heard from the group. Garret hadn't spoken to her in a while, but every time she passed him between classes, he was deep in conversation with his new friend, Trent.

Trent was an Apprentice level warrior. He had dark skin, and always wore jeans and the ugliest sweater Lydia had ever seen. The two were practically inseparable. Lydia remembered when she and Rani had been like that. Tears pricked her eyes, and she wiped them away with the back of her hand.

She had just gotten finished with Battle class when one of the sword fighters ran up to her. It was Trent. He handed her a note and walked quickly away, as if he didn't want to be seen near her. She opened up the folded note, smiling slightly when she saw Garrets sloppy writing.

Lydia,

Meet us by Orange Gym tonight at midnight. Bring anything you can't survive without for a few weeks. Tell no one about this!

Garret, Trent

Late that night, Lydia snuck out of her room, her grey backpack slung over her shoulder. It was heavy with books and clothes. Her sword was attached to a utility belt full of any tools she might need. It clanked louder than she would have liked as she walked down the halls, but she made it to the Orange gym by five past midnight.

Garret was there, his backpack on the floor by his feet. His sword was strapped over his back, and his face was the most determined thing Lydia had ever seen. She had only ever seen a smile across his face, and now, he looked years older. He looked at her, at the smile reappeared. Trent stood next to him, a red backpack on his back. A bronze-colored dagger was strapped to his leg, and it made him look tougher than normal, even though he still wore an ugly gray sweater with a Charlie Brown style stripe across it, which was the same color red as his backpack.

"You ready?" Garret asked, his voice a soft whisper.

"Where are we going exactly?" asked Lydia. She wasn't used to breaking rules, and even though a set of rules had never been laid down, she was pretty sure being out of bed in the middle of the night, planning to run away broke any unspoken rules.

"To go get the missing Clessi," said Trent.

"And to rescue Rani." Said Garret.

"Are you mad? We could be killed, or worse, if we do survive, we'll be in a ton of trouble! We'll miss schoolwork, and-"

"And Rani will be safe." Garret said.

And so, a half hour later, the three of them were following the train tracks, hoping to reach the town by morning. The night air was cool and the only sound around was the crunch of their feet on the gravel. Lydia was already panting, but she knew she owed it to her friend.

"I'm coming for you, Rani," she whispered. "I'm coming."

Searching

Lucas had woken up long ago, but Sylvia was still asleep against him, and so he stayed still. She was so peaceful as she slept, without the crease across her forehead, with the corners of her lips slightly upturned in a gentle smile.

Katia and Nolan-a scrawny boy with black hair and light brown eyes- were digging through their bags, looking for something to eat. They were near South Carolina, and the man had gotten off the highway, and Lucas feared that he had reached his hometown; after all, the license plate had said South Carolina. He scanned for other cars, preferably with Georgia license plates, which were nearby and stopped; by he didn't see any that they could get into without being noticed. Katia's ears twitched and she looked up from her bag. She focused her eyes, hazel eyes with a slit down the middle, like a cat's instead of a human's, on Sylvia.

"Wake Sylvia." She said. Lucas shook her gently, and Sylvia's eyes fluttered open. She looked at Lucas's watch, and the crease cross her forehead reappeared. She took out her side braid and redid it, scowling.

"Why didn't you wake me sooner?" She asked, annoyed.

"You're so pretty when you sleep," Lucas said, and Sylvia turned to Katia.

"There was no need to until now." She said. "But the man is on the phone with his wife, and he is telling her that he is fifteen minutes from home,"

Sylvia peeked her head over the side of the truck. "When we get to the red light," Sylvia said, "We'll get off."

"In heavy traffic?" Nolan asked, his mouth full of crackers.

"We don't have any other options," said Sylvia. She gathered up the stuff they had strewn all over the back of the truck and packed it in the bags. The car slowed, and the crouched.

"On three," she said, "One, two, three!" the leapt of the pickup, and ran for the side of the road. Drivers honked and yelled, and the man looked at them, confused. They ran into the nearest place, a fast food restaurant.

They sat down, and Katia pulled on a blue beanie over her head, hiding her ears. Even though she knew people couldn't see them, she was still paranoid. She grabbed a wallet from her bag and started to get up to order food, and Sylvia grabbed her arm.

"Where did you get the wallet?" She asked.

"That man I bumped into on the way in here," She said. Sylvia sighed.

"Katia, you know that we aren't supposed to do that."

"Old habits die hard," Katia said as she walked up to the workers to order. Sylvia sighed. Katia had been on the streets before coming to the school, since her dad was a Mutant, and her mom was a human, who had somehow seen her ears and drover her out. She had been on the streets since she was five, and had stolen a lot over the years.

Katia slid back into the booth minutes later, holding a tray of food. A salad for Sylvia, burgers for the boys, and a bowl of steaming Chile for herself.

"Chile?" asked Nolan. "At a fast food restaurant?"

"Don't judge," said Katia, searching for the spoon.

"She did buy us food." Said Lucas, and Sylvia glared at him.

"She stole money to buy us from food," she spat.

"Same thing," said Katia. The table smiled, but Sylvia looked at them murderously, like she was going to stab them all with the plastic fork she was using to eat her food. Katia laughed and opened up her spoon, snapping the handle off as she did.

"Awww," she said, looking sadly at her decapitated spoon. Laughter filled the table, and even Sylvia smiled slightly.

Lucas stared out the window at the parking lot. There was a Semi truck outside, and he strained to read the license plate. Georgia.

"What are you looking at?" asked Sylvia, looking up at her boyfriend. He was a few inches taller than her, and it made a funny sight to see a tall girl such as herself having to look up to someone.

"Our ride,"

Trapped

Rani sat in a heap, leaned up against the cages wall. She was high above the ground, but fear of height was the least of her worry. Her leg had a deep gash across it, deep and infected. She hadn't had food in two days, and her stomach growled angrily. She wasn't alone. She was in a warehouse, dark, creepy, and cold, the perfect place for a Superior hideout.

She was in a large birdcage-like cell. A huge iron lock was on the door. A rusty chain held her nearly fifty feet above the ground. There must have been three dozen chains like hers, each with another cage ten feet further down the chain, but she was at the top, she even if she managed to escape, she was trapped. Every day, more and more Clessi filled the cages, but Rani was glad to see that Lydia and Garret weren't among them, even though she missed them like crazy. She missed Garret's quirky grin, and big forest green eyes. She missed Lydia teasing Garret gently, and mainly, she missed being able to talk to her friend.

The cage twisted slowly, and Rani felt her headache coming back. She crawled to the middle of her cage and laid down, staring at the ceiling. She had carved tallies into the floor next to her using the tip of her lightning bolt necklace. She felt the bumps of rust along the bottom of the cage, and the grooves that she had carved. Her hair was loose, and she was using the ponytail tie to cut off the circulation to her leg. The gash was just below her knee, and she moved it up, raising it. She couldn't remember if that was for swelling or infection, so she did it anyways.

The cage moved faster in circles, and she felt seasick. For eight days she had been spinning, and her head pounded. If there as anything left in her stomach, she would have defiantly thrown up. She wondered if anyone was looking for her. Would Lydia and Garret try to find her, or did they think she was dead? She hated to think about it, but the more she did, the more likely it seemed that she was on her own to try to get out of there. She rolled onto her stomach and started shaking the bars, trying to find a loose one. She gritted her teeth, keeping her head level and calm. Crying wouldn't solve anything, and neither would nursing her injured leg without any supplies. She pulled and twisted against the bars.

"I'll make it out of here," She whispered to herself. "Even if I die trying."

*   *   *

Garret, Lydia and Trent rode in the van in silence. They had been hitchhiking for nearly two hundred miles, and they had no idea where they were going. Garret had heard his dad talk about Superior bases to Andrew. There was one in nearly every major city across the states. As soon as they had one in Washington, D.C., they had planned to start trying to 'overtake' the humans then. This always made Garret laugh. Humans were far too stubborn to be taken over. Even though their guns might be useless against them, and so would chemical warfare, they weren't resistant to bombs or fire. Enough bullets would eventually kill a Clessi, but it was like throwing rocks at humans. Clessi could also be crushed, Garret though as they rode on. If you dropped something heavy on them, they would be crushed as well as a human.

The van pulled over, and they climbed out into a small town. The waved goodbye to their ride, and Garret pulled Andrews old phone out of his bag. Andrew hadn't told his dad he had lost the old phone yet, so it still got Andrew's emails. Garret scrolled through them, searching for ones from his dad. He looked for names, cities, anything. He stopped at one email. It read:

Andrew,

The new ones are going to Georgia's place. We are out of room down here.

Garret looked down at it, and his face lit up. "Georgia!" he said.

"There are in Georgia?" asked Trent.

"No, Georgia is a person, not a place. Georgia's my cousin. She's twenty-seven, very nasty, and very powerful. Perfect Superior material."

"Where is she?" Lydia asked.

"I don't know." Said Garret. He opened up the internet, and looked on. He searched for Georgia Valen. Nearly a hundred results came up, but he knew what he was looking for. She was the twenty third result. He opened her Facebook account and searched out her address. It was near New York City.

'New York City has a huge base of operations," he said. "It only makes sense that they would be there," Lydia smiled at him.

"Good job. Now how do we get there?"

Attacked

Flashlights lit up the dark truck interior. The group had set them on boxes, and taped them down to keep them from sliding to the ground. They had spread blankets out on the metal floor, and sat close together. It was cold, and Sylvia guessed that snow probably fell outside, but it was warm enough in the truck. Most of them were sleep by now, but Sylvia wasn't. She stayed awake, listening to the sound of the wind outside of the truck. She could hear other vehicles, and knew they must be on a highway. Something was nagging at her. Something felt utterly wrong, and she didn't like it. Maybe it was nerves, she thought, or maybe it was the feeling of uselessness that was beginning to invade her. She had always been a natural leader, and now that feeling was slipping away all because there was something real to lose. The stakes were higher. And that made all the difference.

They rode well into morning, and sometime around midnight, Sylvia fell fast asleep. In the morning, she was still sound asleep when the others awoke. They laid Sylvia to the side when the man stopped at a rest stop, and walked outside to investigate their surroundings.

It was bright outside, and Lucas had to shield the light from his eyes. They were north of Atlanta still, but they were a lot closer. Lucas looked around, stretching his legs. He was about to run into the bathroom when he heard Katia call his name.

He ran over to her, and found her and Nolan back to back, weapons drawn. Six Superiors surrounded them, each with their own weapons out. Lucas clicked open the thick metal tube inside his pocket, which extended to be a four foot long metal pole, sharpened like a spear at one end. He twirled it threateningly in front of him, joining his comrades at the middle of the group. The Superiors inched closer before attacking the group. Lucas took on one rather large man, while Katia took on two. They were practically in shock. To those who had never seen Katia in action, it was quite terrifying. She had cat-like agility, and took it quite literally. She would pounce, leap, and hiss like a cat when she got into her "zone".

Using a small bronze-colored dagger, she stabbed the one in the chest while ducking under the others blade. Leaving the knife behind, she leapt onto the other Superior, wrapping her arms around their neck. First they turned red, then a soft purple, before falling forward and onto the ground. The other Superior, with a knife still in their chest, swung wildly at her with their sword, cutting a scratch across her arm. Katia hissed in warning, but the Superior had her weapon.

Nolan was attempting to fight off two at once as well, but wasn't doing nearly as well as Katia. If the one Superior had had a weapon instead of club that he was trying to use to knock him out. He slashed out with his sword, cutting gashes on the Superior's chest. The Superior lunged forward, grabbing Nolan's arm. He sunk to the ground in agony as he felt his skin begin to burn as if the Superiors hands were acid.

Lucas was on his knees, cuts all across his arms and chest. His shirt was in tatters, and blood began to ooze from the cuts. The Superior he was fighting was grayish brown, and covered in sharp bumps all over that cut like razor blades. Lucas tried swinging his spear, but it simply slid across its rough skin, sending out sparks. Lucas closed his eyes waiting for the final blow. He waited. And waited. He opened his eyes, and could hardly believe his eyes.

Sylvia stood on the top of the semi, bow raised, arrow notched. She let out the first arrow, taking out the Superior in front of him. Lucas watched, unbelieving, as the Superior that had been about to kill him fell, the chink in his armor found. She launched another, taking out the one that was standing over Nolan. Lucas just gaped as he watched her take out each Superior with deadly accuracy. He had never seen her expression so grim and serous, and he had seen her in battle before. This was different.

One of the Superiors started throwing something, and she did a front flip off the front of the truck, landing crouched. She straightened up, launching two more arrows, taking out another Superior. Three arrows later, and every Superior around them was on the ground. Sylvia stalked over to Lucas, raving mad.

"Lucas Pine, How dare you!" she spat bitterly. "You could have been killed!"

Lucas let out a sheepish grin. " I know," he admitted.

"Why," Sylvia added, "Did you do it then?"

"We didn't know there was any danger when we left you asleep on the truck." Lucas tried, but Sylvia was still mad. She walked back to the truck, her long braid centered straight down her back.

"I love you!" Lucas called after her, but Sylvia wasn't in the mood for listening.

*   *   *

Rani sat on the metal floor of the cage, carving in another tally. It screeched something awful, but no one really cared. She could hear a scuffle below her, and she knew that someone else was being dragged off. Rani didn't know exactly what they did to them once they were gone, but it sounded bad. She could hear screams of protest, and sometimes even screams of pain.

Rani crawled over to the cage cell bars, and started wiggling the loosest one. She figured if she did this every day, soon, it would rust out, and she could use it as a weapon as she escaped. Suddenly, the Chain her cage was on started shaking like crazy. Rani rolled away from the loose bar, afraid that someone would discover it and take it away.

Rani breathed heavily, lying against the bottom of the cage. Her cage shook violently suddenly, and Rani looked over and scooted backwards. A tall man was clinging onto the side of the cage, unlocking her door. It swung open, and he walked inside. Rani hardly had a second before her hands were handcuffed in front of her. Stupidly, she tried to shock him, but the handcuffs tightened on her wrists until she stopped and cried out in pain.

"They have a rather unfortunate tendency to do that," said the tall man. Rani looked him over. He was skinny, with a pristine white lab coat all except for some dry red spots that Rani doubted was ketchup. His eyes were dark black, and it was like looking into utter darkness. His eyes were like looking into black holes, and Rani felt all hope, energy, and strength drain away from her as she looked at him longer. His hair was black, and greased back, slick and greasy looking. Rani looked away from his face and studied the floor. She saw a hand reach out and pull her to her feet. She pushed him away.

"Don't touch me," she said. She knew what was going on. She was being dragged away.

"I give the orders here, not you, little missy." He said, and with the click of a button on his watch, the silver handcuffs tightened, and she grunted in a rather un-lady-like manner. She cursed, and he pushed the button again, and it stopped. Rani sighed in relief and rubbed her sore wrists against her leg. She stood on the good leg, holding the other leg off the ground, like a wounded flamingo.

The man grabbed her by the arm and pushed her out

of the cage. She screamed for a moment, thinking that she was about to fall fifty feet to her death, but instead, she landed on a metal spiral staircase that she hadn't been able to see from her cage. The man stepped out onto it after her, and pulled her too her feet by the back off her gray sweater. He began to drag her by the neck of her sweater, but Rani kicked him in the leg, nearly backing off the staircase. The cuffs tightened again, and she swore loudly.

The man again started to drag Rani down the staircase, and she looked around franticly. She had no idea what to do. She saw pitiful glances from the others in cages like hers. They looked miserable, as if they couldn't stand seeing another person be dragged away.

Rani knew she two options; Let herself be dragged away, or fight until she was most likely killed. She thought about it until she was only about a dozen feet from the ground. She made up her mind quickly, and acted even quicker. She football tackled the tall man off the staircase, pushing him to the ground. She stopped herself a second before falling, but the cuffs tightened, and Rani fell to her feet, screaming in pain. She rolled off the staircase, landing a few feet from the tall man. The tall man stood up, brushed off his immaculate coat off, and then kicked Rani in the stomach. She moaned, and started coughing. He kicked her again before lifting her by the arm and dragging her towards the dark, shady exit that the others had been dragged out off.

Rani moaned in misery, feeling like she had just

made a scene instead of helping herself. She was too hurt to try again. She was dragged through the door before she could try another desperate gamble.

The room was bright, and Rani had to blink several times to clear her vision. It looked sort off like a hospital room, but scarier somehow. The pristine white floor and walls were stained around the chair that Rani was strapped into. Her arms were held in restraints, and her legs were strapped down. The tall man walked over to a table with a wide assortment off tools. He picked up a pair of vinyl gloves and strapped them on.

Rani gulped. This was what happened to Clessi that were dragged away. They were dissected. But to her surprise, the doctor didn't pick up a saw or a knife, but instead a bottle of liquid and a needle. The liquid was pale blue, and seemed to shimmer as it moved. He poured it into the needle being very careful not to touch any of it. Rani gulped. If he wasn't willing to touch it, it seemed dangerous to have it injected inside of her. He picked up and alcohol wipe. He walked over to Rani. Fear burned inside of her like a thirsty fire, but she kept it at bay. She didn't feed the fear inside of her, and tried to replace it with hope. *Maybe it would heal her leg. After all, you never know*, she thought.

Oh wait, Rani thought, *he dragged me down a series of stairs, kicked me in the gut, and made handcuffs nearly slice her hands off. I do know. I'm going to die.*

Rani told her brain to shut up, but it was too late. It

had feed the fear inside off her, and she started to lose control of it. The tall man rubbed the alcohol pad on her arm. It was cold, and Rani shook with fear and cold. The straps securing her leg rubbed against her gash, and she bit her lip to keep from crying. She could feel blood start to flow on her leg, but the tall man didn't seem to care.

He stuck the needle into her arm, and Rani's first thought was *Hey, this isn't that bad. It hurts as much as a flu shot.*

That was before the liquid was injected into her veins. The second it was, Rani screamed. She couldn't help it. It was like fire in her bloodstream, and it spread throughout her, burning every cell she had. She screamed, tears running down her face. Electricity crackled around her, and the handcuffs tightened, but Rani couldn't even feel it. It was nothing compared to the pain that was slowly engulfing her body. The pain grew to blinding, blood roared in her ears, and she blacked out.

Traveling

Trent, Garret and Lydia were sitting close together, worried. The bus ride was bad enough, but they had all seen the Superior board the bus. He was sitting near the front, and knife strapped to his leg. He was waiting for them to try and get off, and they knew it. After that, he would simply get off after them and kill them, or kidnap them, and honestly, they didn't know which was worse. Garret had told the others about the experiments, and now not only were they concerned that these were happening to Rani, but they were worried that these would happen to them if they got off the bus.

"I have an idea," Trent said, "but it's completely mad."

"No one else seems to have one," Lydia admitted, "So go ahead."

Trent explained, and two minutes later, Trent was walking up the bus aisle, using his ability. He was bending the light around himself, so no one could see him. Several pills were in his hand, drowsy Tylenol, which Lydia had had in her utility belt. When the superior looked distracted, he slipped the water bottle out of his bag, and poured the crushed pills into the water, shaking it gently until dissolved. Thankfully, the light bending extended over the water bottle, and so no one saw a floating water bottle in the aisle.

He slipped it carefully back into the Superiors bag

and walked slowly back down the aisle, stepping carefully over bags and peoples legs. He became visible again once back in his seat, to the amazement of a small child behind them, who gasped. Trent winced. His cover had been blown by a four year old. The kid blinked several times before staring, bewildered at his juice box, as if it was causing hallucinations. Trent sighed in relief.

"It's done," Trent murmured to the other two, who nodded. It was a full thirty minutes before the man took a sip of his water bottle, and another thirty before he finished it. It was only ten minutes after that, though, he was fast asleep. They got to the last stop, and climbed off the bus, carefully avoiding the sleeping man at all costs. The bus rolled away without problem.

Lydia pulled out a road map and pointed to their location. "We are here," she said, pointing to a spot nearly a hundred miles from the reed 'x' of the base. "We still have a ways to go."

Garret sighed. "We need to hurry. If we are too late, and" his voice cracked, and Lydia looked at him curiously. *Perhaps,* she thought, *Rani means more to him than he'll care to admit.*

Trent pointed to a car rental company down the road. "What about that?" he asked.

"Do you know how to drive?"

"Fair point." He admitted.

"What about another bus?" asked Garret, but Lydia looked at him as if he was stupid.

"No more buses," she said. "Not again."

"Ok then, what else can we do?"

Lydia smiled, the kind of look that made Garret nervous, and he rarely felt nervous.

"You've got that look," he noted nervously, and Lydia looked at him funny.

"What look?" She said innocently.

"The look that tells me you have a dangerous idea," Garret said simply, looking away down the street to hide his smirk. He had that look a lot, the look that was a brilliant plan and a stupid one at the same time.

"Have you ever heard of boat tours?" Lydia asked.

And so, an hour later, they were driving a boat out of the cities harbor and towards NYC. Lydia had convinced the person that the boat was theirs, and that the keys were theirs as well. Trent steered, and Lydia and Garret were sitting in the front, looking out at the statue of liberty on the skyline. It looked so small from there, and Lydia marveled at how small something so big could look.

"Do you think she's ok?" Garret asked, his face unreadable in the fading light.

"Rani?" asked Lydia. Garret nodded, and Lydia leaned back, staring at the skyline. "Probably. As long as she didn't do anything stupid,"

Garret looked out at the horizon, watching the orange sun sink slowly under the blue waves. The stars began to come out, and a cool breeze blew slowly across the water.

"What if we get there and we are too late?" Garret asked, leaning back to look at the stars.

"We won't let ourselves be too late." Said Lydia, more determined than she truly felt. What if they were too late? How could she deal with Rani's death? She had bonded more with Rani in three days than she had with anyone she had met at her old school, or in the Safe Zone. She and Rani had just fit into each other's lives perfectly, just like best friends should. Tears pricked Lydia's eyes, and she wiped them away with the back of her hand.

Rani would be alright. She had to be. Lydia couldn't accept anything else.

*　　　*　　　*

Sylvia still wasn't talking to Lucas, and she could feel how annoyed he was. She didn't know why he was upset with her; she hadn't done anything rash and stupid to almost get the whole group killed. What if they had found her in the truck? They would have killed her in her sleep, or kidnapped her. Worse, maybe they wouldn't have found her, and she would wake up in the back of the truck, which would have driven away, never knowing what had happened to them. They could have been kidnapped too, or killed on the spot. Sylvia felt she had every right to be mad, and Lucas had none. They sat at opposite sides of the truck, ignoring each other. She missed being able to snuggle up close with him, and feel safe and warm, but the groups safety came first. He would learn his lesson, and then she would see about them. She wished she could get into Lucas's head, and see what he was thinking. Was he sorry, or did he think she was being a cold-hearted child? She longed to know.

The truck took a sharp corner, and they all slide to one side of the truck. Sylvia ended up on top of Lucas. She pushed off of him and scooted back into the corner she was sitting in. She pretended to be studying the golden locket around her neck. The initials R. E. M. were carved into it, and inside was a baby photo of the little curly-haired brunet with pretty cobalt blue eyes that she called her sister. Would her sister even remember her? Would she even know her name? Did she even know that she was still alive? All of these were passing through Sylvia's mind before the truck made another sharp turn, this time sending everyone over to her side of the truck. Lucas slammed into her, sending her sprawling into a wall. Sylvia shoved him off of her, Lucas looked at her with big puppy dog eyes. She sighed and looked into them, trying not to blush.

"Via," he started, and Sylvia already felt her anger subsiding. He was the only person in the world other than her dad to call her Via, and she remembered why she trusted him enough to tell him about the nickname. All the good battles. All the victories. All the nights that they had snuck onto the roof to sit together and look at the stars while holding hands. Lucas brushed a stray hair from her face and tucked it behind her ear. His hand paused, staying on the edge of her face, and she put her hand on top of his, looking into his eyes. His hand was warm under hers, and she sighed.

He opened his mouth to say something, to apologize, but Sylvia cut him off. "I know," she said. He leaned forward and kissed her, and Sylvia gave in to her softer side.

"I'm sorry I yelled." She whispered. "I just couldn't bear to lose any of you."

"And I couldn't bear it if I lost you," Said Lucas, holding Sylvia's hand.

Nolan and Katia smiled at each other. It was like World War III when Lucas and Sylvia fought, actually, it was like World War III when Sylvia fought anyone, especially a Superior. She was the most talented girl the two of them had ever met. She hadn't missed with a single arrow in nearly a year. Lucas could live a hundred lives and never deserve her.

The Experiment

Rani awoke in her cell. The handcuffs were gone, but red cuts around her wrists proved to her that they had been real, and she hadn't just dreamed the whole thing up. Her entire body ached like she had been hit by a truck, and her leg burned. She sat up, moaning at the movement, and looked down at her leg. It was bandaged, but fresh blood soaked through the white cloth. Rani looked over at her arm, where the needle had been injected, and tears stung in her eyes. The whole area around it, and entire two inches, was swollen like a gigantic bee-sting. She moaned, grossed out by the sight. Her arms and legs felt stiff as she tried to use them, and she could see her veins-purple and blue-crisscrossing through her arms. The sweater had been removed, and as she tried to sit up, she realized this, and noticed she was only wearing her jeans and white t-shirt. Her head spun, and she thought for a moment that she would through up.

Whatever they injected into my blood stream, Rani thought, *didn't kill me. I don't think it was meant to.* She pondered this for a second, laying back down on the floor of her cell. She found that her sweater was under her head like a pillow, and she nearly laughed. *They poisoned her, but they were still nice enough to give her a pillow. Unbelievable.*

What was the blue liquid? Was it medicine? Rani gasped as she realized. *She was an experiment. Just like Garret's little sister had been an experiment. That was why so many Clessi here, and most of them young. They were building an army, and they needed the children to be the soldiers.*

Rani tried to sit up again, but fell back against the floor with a thud. She thought about the stairwell. You couldn't see it from the cages, she realized, and she scooted over to the side of the cage and looked down, just to be sure. Rani looked out over the edge, and saw no staircase, even though she knew it was there. She put her hands in her pockets and fished out a penny that had been stuffed to the bottom. She tossed it to the center of the area, where she had last seen the staircase. Sure enough, it landed on the invisible stairs with a metallic clink, and seemed to hover there, suspended in midair.

Grunting loudly, Rani used the bars to pull herself up. Her arms were weak, but she managed to do it soon enough. She started shaking the loose bar again, which was getting just a little bit looser every time, moving just a hair more, and every time, she knew she was a bit closer to freedom.

*   *   *

Lydia was fast asleep on the deck off the ship when she was rudely awaked by a huge wave. It swept over the side of the ship, rocking it dangerously, before splashing its cold seawater onto her. She sat up fast, coughing and sputtering. She could hear Trent and Garret yelling at something, and she wiped the burning salt water out of her stinging eyes before another wave toppled in, sending her sliding across the deck. She looked up, about to yell at Garret, when she saw a Mutant standing on the roof over the steering wheel. Trent was struggling with the wheel, and Garret was slicing away with his sword.

Lydia stood up as fast as she could, holding onto the side of the ship. The deck was slick with the frigid water, and so she went as fast as she could while holding onto the side of the boat.

"Garret, is the water really necessary?" Trent yelled up to him, but Garret just grunted. Lydia was almost to the roofed in area when she got her first good look at the Mutant.

It was tall, bluish skinned, and looked more like a fish than a human to her. It had scales like a fish, and fin like structures on its head, but yet it leapt at Garret and tried to bite him with the force of a shark. Lydia saw the razor sharp teeth and felt her knees go weak, and she slipped on the deck and slid onto the ground. Lydia drew her sword from her bag, which was lying in a puddle, and struggled to stand up again. She walked shakily over to the roof area, and climbed up the ladder on the side.

On the top was a little dryer, and Lydia found footing much easier. Garret was sweating hard, and The Mutant appeared to be pulling ahead in the battle. Lydia ran up from behind and sliced at its back weakly, but it cut a gash through the Mutants back, drawing blood. It roared and turned around, which gave Garret just enough time to regain his footing and begin to attack again. A huge wave crashed over the ship, and Lydia slipped, clinging onto the ladder to keep from falling.

When the water hit the Mutant, it roared, and Lydia saw the wound on its back fade slightly.

"Garret!" she screamed, but her voice was lost over the sound of the crashing waves. Lydia climbed down fast, and ran to her bag. She dug through it, salt water soaking both her and all of her stuff. She found the item she was looking for, and clenched it victoriously in her hand. She put it between her teeth and climbed back up the ladder, clinging on as the ship pitched and rolled.

Once she was on top, she dropped her sword to the ground and took the item out of her mouth. It was small, and plastic. She clicked open the top, and clicked the button. A small flame appeared out of the top. Lydia was holding a lighter.

"What the heck are you doing? Garret screamed over the sound of the waves. "Are you mental?"

"Quite the opposite," Lydia called back, and she brandished the lighter at the Mutant. It turned around, seeing movement out of the corner of its eye. It saw Lydia, and the lighter, and made a sound like a wounded Rhino. It backed away from her, and Lydia walked at it, holding it in front of her.

The lighter stayed light, despite the ocean spray coming at them, and the Mutant backed up further. Garret charged at it, slicing open a gash across its stomach.

"No!" Lydia screamed, but the Mutant fell back into the ocean. A wave swept over them, and the Lighter went out.

"What were you thinking!" Garret spat angrily at Lydia. "You could've died!"

"That Mutant was strengthened by water and weakened by fire. It was in a book I read while we were in the Safe Zone. It's a theory that all mutants have a weakness and strength, and that they are complete opposites. Fire and water." Lydia said calmly, but then her face darkened. "But by shoving it into the water, you healed it. Now it will lie in wait until it feels like attacking."

The sea around them began to stop, and the ship gently drifted for a few seconds before speeding off towards the city once more. The city was much closer now, and the whole skyline was taken up by the tall buildings.

Garret and Lydia climbed down from the roof of the boat and into the steering area with Trent. His ugly sweater was soaked, and his face was dripping wet, but otherwise, he was fine. Garret had a bite out of his arm, and Lydia grabbed it and pulled it up.

"Ow !" Garret complained, but Lydia didn't listen. She pulled him over to her back, taking out her utility belt and strapping it around her waist. She unzipped one of the pockets, taking out gauze and a tub off medical ointment. She spread the ointment over the gash and started wrapping the injury tightly.

"What would you do if I weren't here?" Lydia murmured, mostly to herself.

Garret grinned through the pain. " Bleed to death?" he suggested, and Lydia smiled.

"You probably would," She said, still wrapping her patient's arm with the bandage.

"Do you think Rani is still alive?" Garret asked, his face suddenly overcome with worry.

"Of course," Lydia said, matter-o-factly.

"I miss her alot," Garret said quietly, almost to himself.

"I really miss her too. She's my best friend." Lydia replied, focusing on bandaging his arm, but she had stiffened up, wrapping Garret's arms a bit too tightly, and he cried out in pain.

"Opps," Lydia said coldly, "my bad."

Not-So Successful Rescue

Sylvia, Lucas, Katia and Nolan stood at the top of a tall warehouse. The breeze gently ruffled through their hair, and their faces were serous, It was quite a bit warmer in Georgia then up in Michigan, but the group didn't feel it. They were completely focused on the task at hand. Saving the lives of the kids trapped inside the warehouse. Katia had her ear up to a crack in the window, and was listening carefully to the conversations going on below.

"Still nothing," said Katia, and Sylvia sat down her legs sore from standing. They had been here nearly an hour, and she was beginning to get sick of standing in silence.

Katia put her ear back to the crack in the window and started listening again. Lucas sat down beside Sylvia, putting his arm around her shoulders. Even though the rest of the group couldn't see it, Sylvia's tough exterior was breaking, caving in, all because of the enormous stress she was under.

She shook her head, clenching her teeth. The crease on her brow reappeared, and she stood up, her face serous.

"If one of us got captured, and the others followed, wouldn't they have to bring the captured one to where the others were captured?" she said, mostly to herself, before turning and ripping apart her backpack, thrusting random items out onto the roof. She grabbed a length of nylon cord, and tied one end of it securely to the window hatch on the roof. She tied the other half around her waist.

"Sylvia!" Lucas said, reaching out to grab her hand, but she had already lowered herself down, and was only holding onto the edge with her hands. "That's a thirty foot drop! It could kill you!"

"So could the flu," Sylvia said, before letting go off the edges, letting herself free fall for thirty feet, downwards, before the rope caught, and jerked her violently to a stop. She cried out in pain, as the cord must have dug into her. She used the end of an arrow to start filing away at the rope. She still had another twenty feet before she got to the ground, and the only way to get there was from falling again.

Lucas tried to start to pull her up by the rope, but it was too late. She sliced through the last of the rope, falling to the concrete below hard, landing feet first, but her legs gave out after the fall, and she slammed into the ground. She lay, motionless, on the ground for a few moments, the longest moments of Lucas' life. He had no way of telling if she was dead or alive.

But then she moved her arm, and then sat up, and Lucas let out a sigh of relief. He had never been so happy to see anything in her entire life. Sylvia sat up, rubbing her rope burned waist and bruised legs. Aching, she stood up, her bow and arrows in their quiver strapped safely to her back. She looked around, and the guards around her looked at her in surprise.

"Well, don't just stand there, get her!" one rather big

looking one yelled, and they took out some strange looking guns. The looked like a normal gun, but instead of bullets, they had silver and mechanical beads that looked rather painful to Sylvia.

The shot at her, but when they hit, they weren't normal bullets. They were electrically charged, and the first one let out volts in her body, and the room got fuzzy for her. Dots danced in front of her eyes, and she wearily raised her bow, pretending to try to fight back.

The second and third one hit her arms, and she fell to her knees. The room, already fuzzy, started to spin slightly, and she closed her eyes and calmed her mind. She fell to the floor, not quite out cold yet, but very close. She felt a shoe press into her arm, and she willed herself not to make any movements. She forced herself to stay limp and to keep her eyes closed.

She felt herself being dragged by the arms, and she forced herself to keep her eyes closed. She bit her lip hard, hoping that pain would help drag her out of the fuzzy, dizzy world that the pellets that the guns had shot had put her in. Surprisingly, it worked, and her head started to clear little by little until she felt herself lifted up and into something. Judging by the sound her body made when it smacked against the floor, she was in something big and metal. She was lifted again, put in a seat, and strapped down. Her hands were tied with something, probably a zip tie, and lay in front of her, limp and useless. She heard a door slam shut, and something loud filled her ears with its roaring. She carefully opened one eye just a crack, to make sure she was alone.

She looked around, and seeing that no guards seemed to be around, she opened her eyes. She was on a plane, a very old propeller plane, and in every seat was a kid to young adult, all strapped in with the seat belt, their wrists zip tied shut. They were all unconscious, their heads laid against their chests or the seat. Sylvia tried to reach around for her bow and arrows, but they were gone.

The plane was very old, and all the seats were ripped and smelly. Most of the interior was brown and tan, and very plain.

Sylvia spotted a box near the front of the plane, and she could see the tip of an arrow from the edge. She moved her wrists back and forth, wiggling slowly, pulling one tiny notch of zip tie open more and more every time, until they were just big enough to slid off over her wrist. She pulled it off with her teeth and undid her seat belt. She tip toed to the front, grabbing her bow and quiver full of arrows from the box. She peeked through the curtain beyond the box, into the cockpit. There were two men driving the plane, and then two others, sitting behind them. Sylvia guessed that they were body guards.

As she watched, she could see that they were all heavily armed, and started to back away slowly. She walked back to her seat, and then heard a door pop open. It was hard to hear over the roar of the engines, and Sylvia guessed they were about to take off. She sat down, buckled herself in, and hid the arrows and bow under her seat. She slumped down, pretending to be out cold.

Lucas, Katia and Nolan had opened the back hatch of the plane, and were tiptoeing towards the nearest empty seats. They had seen Sylvia being dragged onto this plane, and had hopped on after taking care of few guards. For such a big threat, they had truly terrible security.

Katia walked over to Sylvia and tapped her lightly on the shoulder. Sylvia turned and looked at her, smiling at her friend. She silently unbuckled, and stood up, bringing her group together in the back of the plane.

"We have to stay quiet," she whispered. "There are two pilots and two guards, all heavily armed. They are going to bring us to wherever the rest of the kids are. You guys are going to hide in here, and let them take me away. I'm going to hide my Swiss army knife so that I can get out of any cage they put me in. You guys are to quietly get everyone else out. This has to go off without alerting anyone of our presence. If Valen is at that base with all of the kidnapped, and he tries to stop it, I bet my bow that we'll be dead, or worse."

Nolan was investigating a pile of silver boxes in the corner, and Sylvia shot him a dirty look.

"Nolan!" she hissed, " Don't touch anything!" Nolan shrugged and open up one of them.

They all gathered around it and looked inside. The inside was padded heavily, and was filled with vial after vial of liquid. Most of the liquid was red, but some was gold, or silver, and three or four were blue.

"What do you think it is?" Katia asked, lifting one silver vial very carefully out of the box.

"Don't touch it!" Sylvia whispered but Katia held it carefully in her hands, her cat eyes wide in excitement. She ran her finger carefully along the edge, reading what the label said.

"Specimen 24, Category C Mutant blood." She read out loud, and Sylvia gasped.

"Category C?" she said in wonder. "They only go up to D!"

"D?" asked Nolan.

"Dangerous," Lucas said, "Extremely dangerous. Practically impossible to kill."

"So a C is like what?" Nolan asked. "Cuddly?"

"C doesn't stand for anything. All of the one's we've ever fought have been Category A. We fought one Category B, but only once. A Mutant Category C or a D would kill us in about three minutes flat." said Sylvia, staring in fascination.

"So the fact that they have the blood of a Category C means that they are very, very powerful." Said Lucas, staring at the vial. Katia slid it carefully back into the case. She slid out one of the gold vials and read the label. She gasped, nearly dropping it.

"What?" Nolan asked. "Is it a Category D?"

"No" said Katia, going pale. "Nightmare blood."

The group slid away from the vial of gold blood as the plane took off. Katia held it firmly in her hand, holding tightly, but not so to break it.

"Nightmare blood?" Asked Sylvia, her voice soft and weak. "I thought that was only a story!"

"Nightmares?" said Nolan, and then he paled. "You don't mean-"

"That is exactly what I mean. This is human blood, taken from them when they were truly frightened. Scared to death, actually. The level of fear that causes Nightmares usually kills the human, but sometimes, they'll transform, being horribly scarred both mentally and physically. They became blood-thirsty, and cause mass murders."

"I thought that you couldn't defeat a Nightmare." Said Katia, looking shocked.

"The last known one was Jack the Ripper, who killed twelve humans and twenty-four Clessi in London before some Mutant finally killed him."

"If they are powerful enough to have nightmare blood,

and several vials of it, then I don't see how we really stand any chance. We really should have been caught and killed or kidnapped on this plane if they are this powerful."

"Maybe they know we are on this plane," Sylvia said softly, "And they are just letting us think we have the upper hand.

Lucas was staring at a vial of red blood, deep in thought. He had hardly spoken a word in over ten minutes, and instead just stared at the vial.

"What does that one say?" asked Sylvia, putting her arm on Lucas' shoulder. He jumped in surprise, then, realizing it was her, let out a crocked grin. Reading the label, though, he frowned again.

"Its human blood," He murmured, confused.

"Let me see," whispered Sylvia, taking the vial from his hand and reading it.

"It says Human, Female, when on Adrenaline." She read, her voice low. "Why would they need Human blood?"

"Why would they need any blood at all?" asked Katia quietly.

"I have no idea," said Nolan, "but take a look at this." He lifted up the layer the vials were standing on, and set it aside gently on the ground. The ground had leveled out now, and the plane was flying at an even angle. Beneath the layer was another layer filled with needles in sterile wrappings. There were nearly fifty of the needles, all wrapped up. Nearby were hundreds upon hundreds of alcohol pads.

"They are planning on injecting it," Sylvia whispered. She picked up a vial of the blue liquid. It was light, shimmering with light. It practically glowed. She read along the side, and her face went deathly pale. "Oh my god." She said, covering her mouth. "Oh my god."

"What is it?" asked Katia, her voice very, very quiet.

"It's waste." Sylvia said. "Toxic waste. The Toxic Waste. Straight from the leakage during the twenties."

"But why do they have all of this stuff?" asked Nolan excitedly, and Sylvia shushed him.

"Quiet," Sylvia whispered.

"Why do they have all of this stuff?" Nolan asked again, this time whispering.

"I have no idea," Sylvia admitted softly.

"Is it medicine?" asked Katia softly.

"No, it's the opposite of that." Sylvia muttered. "But it's not poison."

"What else could it be?" asked Katia, murmuring mostly to herself. She ran her fingers absent mindedly through her hair, pausing when she got to her ears.

"Mutant blood." She said. "Mutant blood!"

"What is it, Katia?" Sylvia asked.

"I'm a half mutant half human!" said Katia.

"Yes, so?" Sylvia said. "I've known that for years, and so have they."

"How do they make half Mutant half Humans?" asked Katia. "Mutants and humans don't exactly fall in love!"

"Oh my god!" said Sylvia, covering her mouth. "Katia, you're a genius!"

"What?" asked Nolan, lost.

"They are experimenting. Making Clessi and Humans into Superiors and Mutants. They're building an army."

*   *   *

The room was all dark except for the light that poured in from the one glass window overlooking a large warehouse filled with cages, suspended by huge metal chains. Valen leaned back in the large office chair deep in thought.

The door swung open, and a tall figure walked in, a pristine white lab coat swishing behind him.

"Doctor," Valen greeted the man coldly.

"You were right about that girl," the tall man with the

dark eyes said. "She's survived five hours so far,"

"Her father survived well at first too," Valen said, sitting forward. "And then he went Mutant,"

"She is strong, and young," the doctor said looking out over the cages. "we've perfected the formula since then. She'll be the perfect weapon."

"How do you plan to control her?" Valen said, standing up and walking to gaze out the window. Rani was laying at the bottom of the cage several feet away, unconscious. Even through the wall, he could hear the crackle of electricity in the air. It jumped like lightning between the bars on her cage. "I've only met her once, but she was quite the spitfire. Stopped my heart for a minute even at normal power. Killed a dog too," he said. "Of course, I doubt she even noticed. She couldn't control her power."

"We don't need to control her," the tall man said. "Just to destroy her. Drive her to the brink of insanity, then let her loose in a world that will be terrified of her. Humans destroy what they don't understand. She'll fight back. She won't know what she can do yet. And then she'll level entire cities with one strike. But she's a ticking time bomb. Her body can't handle it for long. Give it two months. She'll burn out, taking a small city with her. She's a grenade, you just have to be out of the way when she explodes."

Closer Together

Rani sat up, her entire body soaked in sweat, although she was freezing cold. She was shivering like mad, and was panting. Her arms ached, and she remembered shaking the bar until she had passed out. Her veins were all dark grey, and the spot on her arm was nearly three times as big. Rani felt tears running down her face. Whatever the shot was, it was defiantly poisonous. It was killing her, slowly but surely. She wondered if this was what Garret's little sister felt like. In so much pain, all the time, but not feeling weak by any means. She felt strong, like she could rip apart the cage with her bare hands if she wanted too.

But Rani didn't want to. She just wanted to sleep, and escape the pain for a while. She knew what she should be doing. She should be working on escaping, but it was too painful. Everything hurt. Breathing hurt. Thinking hurt. Moving hurt.

Rani laid there, looking at the ceiling working on blinking without wincing in pain. She heard the cell door opened, and it squealed loudly, as if magnified by a microphone. She winced, trying to cover her ears, but not able to get her hands to ears. She saw the tall man in the white lab coat standing above her, looking down in disgust.

"Dying, are we?" he said, clicking his tongue in disapproval. "We can't have that, can we?" He reached down another needle full of bright red liquid. He injected it into Rani's other arm, and she screamed loudly, tears pouring down her face.

"Just leave me alone to die!" She screamed, sobbing. "Just let me die!"

"I can't do that. You've survived longer than expected. Most only last an hour. It's been forty nine hours since the first shot. It's a miracle." The man wiped his hands off on his lab coat, disgusted from touching Rani.

"We finally got the formula right. Nine milligrams of Toxic Waste, one milligram of Nightmare-"

"I don't give a crap!" Rani screamed. "Whatever was in it, it's killing me!"

"No, it's doing the opposite. You're going to be truly alive. Completely, truly alive. You'll be living over everyone. You'll be like a god."

"Then I am going to kill you" Rani screamed at him. "You won't do this to anything else!" Rani started to sob, nearly chocking on tears. She hurt all over. She just wanted it to end.

The man looked down at her, a cruel smile across his lips. "No, you won't." He strode out of the cage, his lab coat flapping behind him. Rani sighed, closing her eyes. She felt herself falling, feeling herself slipping down into sleep.

*   *   *

Lydia coughed up the salty, cold seawater, spitting it

out onto the deck.

"Seriously, guys, just once, I would like be without seawater all over me," She said, spitting the seawater out of her mouth.

She could hear Garret and Trent yelling, and she set the book down. She dog-eared the page, something that drove her absolutely crazy, but for lack of a bookmark, she had to. Heaven forbid she lost her place in a book. The sea beast was attacking them again, and she ran unevenly over to her backpack, tripping three times. She took out the lighter, and lit it, the small flame warming her cold fingers. Lydia looked around. It was midday, so she must have been reading longer than she thought. She couldn't help how lost she could get in a book, snuggling into the deepest corners of the pages and the storylines, knowing each character like the back of her hand.

She shivered and rushed over to the beast which was attacking the boys. She waved the lighter at it, and it, screeched loudly, letting Garret go. He sliced at it, cutting a deep wound across its chest. The Mutant screeched, falling backwards onto the deck. Garret sliced at it, killing it.

Lydia tossed Garret the lighter, still lit.

"Do me a favor and burn it this time," she said, "And try to use your brains once and a while instead of your weapons."

Lydia walked back over to the other side of the boat,

taking her book off the deck. It was still dry, even though she wasn't. She opened it up and started to read. The boat rolled with the waves, and sea spray covered Lydia in salty water droplets. She looked up at the sky. It was dark, and the sky was dark gray, the clouds twisting, tumbling and turning overhead. Rain was falling over the city, and as they got closer, it started raining on them as well.

"Garret!" Lydia yelled. "Knock it off!"

"It's not me this time!" he yelled back at her from the front. "I'm not doing anything!"

The rain soaked Lydia's hair, and it clung to her face, and she pulled it back out of her face with a ponytail tie around her wrist.

They drew closer and closer to the city, and the skyscrapers seemed to get taller and taller until they had to crane their necks to see the tops of them. Lydia put her book, soaked, back into the plastic bag more out of habit than anything else. She stared in wonder as she passed the Statue of liberty. She had lived in New York City her whole life, but had never seen the Statue. It was Awe-inspiring to her. It was amazing that she had run so far for so long only to come right back here. She felt like a whole different person. She was completely changed. She was practically nothing like the girl who had left the city almost two weeks ago. She had been a geeky, weak nerd. Now she was a geeky, slightly stronger, Mutant beating, nerdy girl. And that, to her, was all that mattered.

They pulled into the city harbor, parking their boat in a random parking spot, and climbing out. The rain poured down hard, and it was impossible to see more than twenty feet in front of them. Lydia looked around, and saw the clouds spinning overhead. It was almost like the start of a tornado. Garret and Trent didn't seem to notice, though, and so Lydia kept it to herself. Two weeks ago, she would have been all over the strange weather anomaly, but this week it could be a Superior trying to kill them, and Lydia kept her mouth shut. No need to worry the boys.

The walked along the streets, blending in with the other passersby, expect for Trent, whose ugly sweater stuck out like a sore thumb. As they got further and further into the city, Lydia started to recognize the street names. They began walk faster, and Lydia saw her apartment as they walked by. She could see the purple curtains hanging in the window her sister and she had shared for years. She could see her family's orange cat, Cheese-puff, sitting in the same windowsill as always. Lydia smiled as she walked, and the rain began to pour down harder, until she could no longer make out anything about the buildings they passed.

"Do you even know where we are going?" Asked Lydia, shielding the rain from her face.

"Yes," Garret answered. "North Avenue. There's quite a large warehouse there. If they aren't there, then there is another warehouse across the river."

Lightning crackled across the sky, and Lydia felt her

mind wander to Rani again. Could the lightning be caused by Rani? Could she be trying to send them a signal to lead them to her? Lydia was so deep in thought that she didn't see the men walk up behind, the men in the expensive suits holding Tasers in their hands. They grabbed both of Lydia's arms and pulled her into a nearby ally, with her screaming. Garret and Trent ran after her, but she had vanished into thin air, along with the two men.

"Trailers," Garret growled. "I should have known they would show up."

"What are we going to do?" asked Trent. "We can't let them get away with her!"

Garret slipped Andrew's smartphone out of his pocket. It still wasn't disconnected, and he searched through the notes on it quickly, pausing when he saw the thing he was looking for.

"Come on," he said, marching off in the opposite direction.

"Where are we going?"

"Exactly where they are going with Lydia. The Empire State Building."

Finding The Missing

Sylvia had fallen asleep in the seat, the zip tie back around her wrists, but looser than it should have been. Her bow and quiver of arrows were with Katia, where they hid in the back, behind the boxes. They had been trying to figure out why there was human blood, and why each vial of human blood had a different emotion written on it for hours, with no luck. They knew it was probably some kind of an experiment, but why? These thoughts had been twisting and turning around in her head until she had finally fallen asleep. She woke up as the plane landed, and shook violently. She looked around quickly, and seeing that everyone else on the plane who was tied up was still unconscious, or at least, she hoped they were unconscious, and so she closed her eyes and let her head hang against her chest. She heard the engines die, and the men in the front start to get up and walk towards her. *Just keep quiet,* she thought to herself, *please just stay quiet,* she thought, hoping that her friends in the back would. Katia would know to, but Lucas and Nolan were completely unknown. And Lucas was known for doing stupid rash stuff. They were probably doomed.

Sylvia felt herself being lifted up, and she felt herself thrown over someone's shoulder like a sack of potatoes. She nearly grunted, since it felt like being sacked in the gut, nothing she wasn't used to, but she hadn't been expecting. The person walked outside, and the cold air hit her like a brick wall. She felt snowflakes falling on her hair and arms and she shivered slightly, trying her best to stay limp, but failing. The person who was carrying her dropped her onto platform of some kind, and the sound resounded with a loud thud. The object was cold, and metallic, and her face, which lay against it, stung with the cold. She heard something close, and she cracked one eye open carefully.

She was in the back of a pickup truck, and the back had just been shut. There were nine or ten other people in there with her, all tied and unmoving. Someone threw a tarp over them, but it didn't keep out the wind and cold air. The truck started, and started the longest car ride of Sylvia's life. It was so cold that frost started forming on Sylvia's eyelashes and in her hair, and just when she thought things couldn't get any worse, the air warmed a few degrees, and the next second, they had driven into a raging thunderstorm.

Sylvia peeked out of the tarp and watched as they drove across a large bridge. There was a city all around them, a big city, but Sylvia had no idea which one. They could be in Chicago, San Francisco, Orlando, NYC, Toronto, anywhere really. She stared around, looking for any sort of hint to where she was. She watched the road signs until one caught her eye. Brooklyn. She was in NYC. The city that never sleeps. The big apple. The place she had always wanted to see, but under much different circumstances. She had wanted to come here and walk the streets with Lucas, holding hands, going to little coffee shops on dates. She had wanted to go sightseeing. She defiantly had not wanted to see it for the first time tied up in the back of a pickup truck.

The truck drove on for several more minutes, and water found its way underneath the tarp, forming first puddles, then pools of water, until it finally flooded the back of truck, soaking her to the bone. Sylvia wondered if the others had seen her being loaded onto the back of the truck. Were they following her, ready to be her backup? Or were they still in the plane, trying to think up a plan? Or worse, had they been caught, and now kidnapped like her? She simply had no idea.

The truck slowed to a stop, and parked outside a rather large warehouse. It was gray metal, and huge. There was a large parking lot outside of it, and it boarded the ocean. Sylvia could hear the large waves crashing against the concrete breakers. She heard the car's door slam, and she closed her eyes and made herself go limp. Moment later, she was scooped up, and thrown over someone's shoulder once again. She bit her lip hard to keep from grunting. It took every square inch of sheer willpower she had to stay limp, but somehow, she did. She was carried for a minute or two, before she felt herself being carried up a flight of stairs. She heard the metal sequel of a door being opened, and then she was thrown onto the cold metal floor of something.

Sylvia waited until she heard the footsteps fade away, and then she opened her eyes. She was in a large cage, all metal, with bars on the sides and top, and a floor on the bottom. It was roughly circular, more like an oval, and it reminded her of a birdcage. Sylvia sat up and looked around her. She was surrounded by dozens and dozens of cages, all suspended by metal chains from the ceilings. The highest cage was at least fifty feet high, and the lowest was five or six feet off the ground. Sylvia was somewhere in the middle. Sylvia slid the zip tie of her wrists and set it down beside her. She took the knife out from under her shirt, where she had strapped it, sheathed, around her stomach. The guards had never thought to look there, since who would search someone twice, especially if they thought she had been unconscious the entire time.

Sylvia looked around, then crawled over to the cage door. She started working on picking the lock. It was an ancient iron lock, rusted with age, which made it impossible to pick, but rather easy to cut apart. She started working on slicing it apart as she looked around. She could see some Clessi she knew, from her school. A few were lying on the grounds of their cages, looking sick, and others leaned against the sides, looking nearly dead. They looked starved, and most of them had strange lumps on their arms. The ones who didn't looked the most alive. Every few minutes, one random one would start having random convulsions before stopping moving completely. A tall man in a white lab coat would run up to their cage, although Sylvia didn't know how, since he seemed to walk right up the air. Maybe he could fly.

The man would then open their cage and pull them down from it. They didn't even fight him. He brought them to the ground and handed them to some of the guards. With a lump in her throat, Sylvia realized that they were dead. Her little sister could have already died. Sylvia shook away the thought after she became so distracted that she sliced open her thumb with her knife.

What was causing those red marks on their arms? Sylvia thought. *It seemed to be only the ones with the marks that were dying. Were they connected to the vials in any way? Were the vials poisonous, after all? Maybe they were testing weapons on them.*

Sylvia was halfway through the lock now, and her knife had heated up as she grinded it against the metal lock. She was focusing on the Tall man again. He was dragging a perfectly healthy unmarked Clessi boy towards a room. He was doing his best to fight, but failing miserably. He was dragged into the room, and the door was shut. Sylvia stopped cutting and stared at the room. It had been months since she had used her power. It hurt her head so badly, but she used it anyway. Her vision zoomed in on the room, and she looked right through the door. People and Clessi were partly invisible, skin partly transparent, and bones and internal organs visible to her. She always felt sick when she saw people like this, but she couldn't help it. She saw through everything when she used the sight.

The tall man held a needle full of some kind of liquid. It was gold, and Sylvia gasped. He injected it into the boy, who screamed loudly. Sylvia watched the gold race through his bloodstream, turning every organ black and gray, shriveling up as it reached it. When it reached his heart, she saw the boy's feeble heart start to give up. The heartbeat became uneven, and irregular, then faster and faster, like a runaway train, until it finally died, and the boy stopped screaming. The tall man unstrapped the boy and called for the guards. Sylvia read his lips, since she couldn't hear him. The boy was dead. He was asking for them to dispose of the body.

Sylvia leapt back, ripping herself from the sight. She was breathing heavily, and her heart hammered in her chest. They had just killed that boy. They had probably killed many more. Sylvia felt an emotion arise that she hadn't felt in ages. Fear. She hadn't felt true fear in years. Not since she had made it to the Safe Zone. She had been running towards it. She was in a larger group, with seven people total. A Mutant had been chasing them. She had been the only one to make it over the brick wall and into the building. The only survivor. And that's exactly what she had become. A survivor. A fighter. She was a fighter who had a score to settle with Mutants and Superiors alike. Valen had kidnapped her friends. He might have even killed a few. They Mutants had killed a few as well. In her eyes, they were no better than the Mutants. They killed without purpose, just to spill blood. There was no self-defense, so act of preservation of anyone else. It was simple, cold blooded murder. And it made every hair on Sylvia's neck stand on end. Goosebumps covered her arms, and she shook. She hadn't feared since the day she had made it to the Safe Zone because nothing had ever had the danger to make her afraid again. But now she was afraid again.

Sylvia went back to cutting the lock. She could hear cages rattling above her, and the chain started to spin, knocking Sylvia off balance. She stumbled, cursing, then started to cut again.

Many, many cages above her, Rani was shaking the bars. Her arms were strong, and the pain was down. Whatever had been in the shot had really done the trick. The veins were not as gray anymore, and she wasn't sweating and freezing anymore. With each hour, the veins were getting less and less gray and black, and blending back into her skin. She looked almost normal now. She had no way of knowing what her face looked like. Would her eyes look like Garret's little sisters? Would they look like a Mutant's? Or worse, would the look like the tall man's?

She shook the cage, her muscles tightening, and tearing through the metal as if it were paper. She was a monster. She held the bar in her hands, like a weapon. She ripped off the lock, and shoved the door open. She leapt over to where the coin was, marking where the stairs were. She could hear gasps of surprise from the prisoners around her. She wanted to free them too, but she knew it wasn't safe yet. She would let them out when it was safe. She ran down the stairs, muscles rippling in her legs, her long curly brown hair flying behind her as she ran. Her necklaces bounced against her chest, and electricity crackled around her like a thousand tiny fireworks.

She leapt from thirty feet above the ground off the metal stairs and onto the ground, landing crouched, with her fist slamming into the concrete floor. It left cracks, but her hand didn't hurt. She stood up, electricity flashing around her, blue and neon. Guards, armed, ran at her. The first one that reached her tried to run her through with his sword. She set her hand on his chest and sent a wave of electricity through her arm, sending him to the ground. She opened her hands, balls if blue electrical energy forming in each one, moving and growing like flames. She threw them both, hitting two in the dead center of their chest. She threw several more, knocking several more down. Arrows fired at her, but the electrical field around her stopped them in midair. They burst into flame, blue fire, and burned to ashes in the air. Everyone was staring now, including Sylvia. She stared at Rani in surprise. It was the girl who had been kidnapped before making it into the gates. The girl's eyes glowed the same neon blue as the fire around her. Sylvia gasped. *Not all experiments had gone so horribly wrong*, she realized. *Sometimes, they went right, creating her.*

Once the last of the guards who were stupid enough to charge at her had stopped, Rani turned around, staring at the tall man. His eyes were fierce and cold, but Rani was stronger than his power now. Her hair was blowing back as if in some wind that was only affecting her.

"Let them go," Rani said, her voice shaking the warehouse. Lightning lit up the sky around the warehouse. It was only striking around it now, drawn to Rani like a moth to a flame.

"I'm afraid I can't do that," He said, his voice like a blade. He walked forward, unafraid of the power she now held. "You can't hurt me." He held up his wrist. Around it was a bracelet, made of some sort of crystal.

"Quartz crystals. You have Mutant blood in you. Mutants can't fight against the crystal. It's too pure for them." Rani shot balls of blue electrical fire at him, but it vanished into a shower of blue shimmering air as it got within three feet of the man.

"Get back into your cage," he said, a cruel smile across his lips. He took a step forward, and Rani took a step backwards.

"I could still use this strength," she said. "I could snap you like a toothpick. A toothpick."

"You don't have the metal capability to. You still have a bit of human in you, and that bit will keep you from doing it. You don't have the stomach to look me in the eyes and break my back. You would go insane."

Rani was shaking a bit, and she ran her hands through her hair, looking like she was bearing the weight of the world. She turned and leapt, her feet leaving the ground and not touching it again for nearly ten feet. She leapt three times, over towards the small white room, the one that she had gotten the first shot in. She disappeared inside for a few seconds before reappearing. She leapt back to where she was standing before, holding something in her hands. She lifted up so everyone could see it. It was vial of the glowing blue liquid.

"Twenty Milliliters of it," Rani yelled, and the lightning crackled. "That dose is enough to kill anything." She didn't leap at the tall man though, instead holding the needle to her arm. "If I inject this, it'll kill me. You're biggest experiment will have failed. You would lose so much work. You've killed so many for the right formula, but it could only ever work on me. There could be something special about me that has caused me to be different. Are you willing to risk that?"

"You would gain nothing from committing suicide," The tall man said.

"But you would lose everything," she said," and that's good enough for me." She pressed it her arm firmly, and the tall man leapt forward.

"No!" he shouted. Rani relaxed her arm, and the tall man continued. "What do you want from us?"

"I want every person who is being kept captive here set free. I won't drop the needle until I see them safely across the bridge," Rani said, turning her head out the window towards the large bridge. "As soon as they are safe, I will drop the needle, and you can do whatever you want to me. Just let them free."

"How do we know you won't kill yourself anyway?" the tall man asked dryly, and Rani smiled, finally having the upper hand.

"You said it yourself. Suicide is gaining me nothing.

But I will resort to it if necessary."

The tall man looked around, and then stared at Rani. "The decision isn't totally up to me, you know," he sneered. "You are the second person to survive this. We always have her." He pointed, and Rani turned to look. He pointed to a metal door, surrounded by the clear crystals. A guard opened, and Rani looked at Garret's little sister. Her veins were still grayish black, ad her eyes glowed, one green, and the other yellow. She looked more afraid than vicious, though, and Rani felt her heart ache as she looked at her. They reclosed the door, and Rani looked back at the tall man. He smiled, and Rani backed up another step.

"And of course," a voice said, a voice that sounded like ice cracking. The sound of it sent Goosebumps up Rani's arms. "You would have to talk to me to let them go."

Trailers

Trent had seen Garret angry lots of times. Garret had a short fuse, and often flew off the handle. He was mad when he had gotten beaten in a fight back in the Safe Zone. He was mad when upset when Lydia made him look stupid. Garret was mad when someone brought up his father. But Trent had never seen Garret this mad.

Garret was furious. His face was red, hiding the freckles that dotted his cheeks. His normally perfect smile was replaced with his teeth clenched angrily.   Frankly, Trent was terrified by this.

Garret stormed for nearly two miles. Rain had begun to pour down with such force that it stung with welts, and the streets were flooded with traffic, but not a pedestrian was to be seen.

They reached the empire state building in a matter of minutes, which was impressive for having walked so far. Garret strode into the lobby, water dripping off of him. He walked up to the Elevator operator.

"Level 66, now," he barked.

"I'm sorry, but-" Garret leaned over the desk towards the man sitting behind it. He was in his late thirties, with dark skin and graying hair.

"I suggest you let me go up there, or you won't make it

to retirement." Garret paused, before adding, "If you've triggered the silent alarm, I will kill you." The man moved his hand away from the desk nervously. Beads of sweat had begun to form on his forehead.

"Level 66, now," Garret repeated.

"No one is allowed-"

"You just watched some people who were allowed up there drag a young girl up there with them. Her life is in danger. If you have any shred of humanity in you, you will let me save her life," Garret commanded with a tone of finality. The man turned a key in a lock, and the elevator opened.

Trent mumbled a thank you to the man as he clambered into the elevator beside Garret. Garret let his bag drop to the ground as the elevator doors slid closed, and pulled out the bronze colored sword.

Trent did the same, kicking his bag aside.

"What's the plan?" he asked, jogging in place.

"There is no plan."

"Brilliant," said Trent, shaking his head. Garret needed Lydia more than he thought.

The doors slid open, and a short, pudgy man in a black suit leapt at them. Trent sliced at him with his sword, but it slid uselessly across him.

"Garret!" Trent shouted. "They're Human!"

Garret threw his sword aside and swept his arms out in front of him as a loud sound of glass shattering was heard. The entire contents of a fifty gallon fish tank crashed down on the man, glass and fish included.

Trent threw a large chair at another one who came running towards them. He heard a window smash, and looked over just in time to hit the ground as a hurricane strength wave smashed into the group of people rushing towards them.

Trent heard gunshot echoing around them. It was a weird sort of sensation, like being hit by a swarm of bees. The bullets left large welts were they hit. Trent gritted his teeth. Clessi were harder to kill than humans, having stronger skin, healing faster, and other useless facts he had learned in class, but it was strange all the same.

Garret flared his arms out, and Trent closed his eyes as four people were thrown violently out of the broken windows. The gunshots stopped, and the remaining ones put their hands up.

"Backup isn't coming," Garret said, staring down the group a look of pure disgust.

Trent flinched as he heard a huge thunderclaps, shaking the building. The sky outside was pitch black, and the lightning lit up the sky with incredible brightness. It was enough to make anyone stare in awe. The thunderclap shook the building, rumbling loud thunder. Trent had n ever felt so small in his life. He watched as two more strikes electrified the same place. He gaped.

This wasn't a storm.

This was a battle.

Trent turned to tell Garret, but the fury in his eyes silenced him. Trent knew Garret had demolished the bathroom in the second wing of the Safe Zone when he heard the news of Rani. Piping had been blown, and geysers of water had threatened to flood the building. He only slightly less angry now.

"Where is she?" Garret asked wildly, like an animal on the verge of attacking. One of the women dressed in an all-black business suit looked over towards a door to their left. It was all metal, and seemed like it weighed a ton. The two of them ran to it, only to find it locked.

Trent grabbed the door roughly, his fingers digging into the cold metal. He gripped tightly before cleanly snapping the door off of its hinges.

Garret grinned approval at him. "Nice," he said before rushing inside.

Trent grinned back. "It's all leverage," he explained, thinking back to one of the many classes he had sat through while being in the Safe Zone.

The door opened to a long concrete hallway, with iron

cells on either side. People, men women and children laid on the floors in the cells, all miserable, all beaten, and all Clessi. Each of them probably had the power to blow the building, but it was useless now.

Lydia was a few cells in the corridor. Her skin was paler than he had ever seen her, and she was cold as ice. Bruises dotted her arms and on her check. Trent made a strangled sound. If bullets only left welts, he could only imagine what had done this.

Lydia got slowly to her feet, shaking. Her gray eyes were filled with tears.

"Garret," she whispered. Garret and Trent yanked the door roughly, using the same leverage he had used to break the first door. It snapped off roughly, leaving sharp edges, and twisted sides.

Lydia ran out, wrapping her arms around Garret.

Trent cleared his throat, looking over at them.

"That friend of yours," He said, breaking Lydia and Garret apart. "She controls electricity, right?"

Lydia nodded. "Strongest I've ever heard of,"

"That's one hell of a girl." He said, turning to gaze out of the door, towards the broken window. The others turned to look as well.

Outside, black storm clouds circled dangerously, like

vultures circling their prey. Rain poured down, hammering the tops of buildings and roads. The wind whistled like a tornado tore over them.

The lightning was the most impressive however. It shot across the sky, glowing a bright yellow white, spreading out like the veins of a human. It lit up the dark clouds, and reached its long, deadly fingers out toward a lone warehouse near the water. The thunder that followed shook the ground like an explosion, with the sound and force of a bomb.

Lydia stepped forward. The others barely heard her over the crackle and rumble of thunder.

"Rani."

Escaping

Rani turned around slowly, looking up at the giant of a man. He had slicked back black hair, and a long dark trench coat. He stared at her from behind dark eyes. Valen.

"And I don't want you to leave," he said icily. He threw his arms to either side of him, and the concrete shattered into a million tiny fragments of stone. Rani wobbled unevenly, struggling to keep her balance. Valen let out a cold, cruel laugh, and Rani felt the needle rub against her skin. She moved it away from her arm quickly.

The concrete around her shifted, and lifted off the ground, surrounding her in a ball of hovering stones. They crashed to the ground, and they hit Rani as they fell. Her field of blue electricity stopped a few, but some fell through, ripping holes in her little electric bubble. She grabbed a large one and hurled it with all her might at Valen, but he lifted one hand out in front of him, turning it to dust. The dust blew harmlessly by him, and he wiped the remains off of his coat with his hands. Rani lifted one hand out in front of her, and shot a bolt of lightning straight at him, but a wall of concrete rose from the ground and shielded him. She shot ball after ball of electricity at him, only chipping parts of the stone. *I must be using myself up,* she thought.

Rani had beads of sweat on her forehead, and she stopped her electrical attack. They were at a stalemate. He really didn't want Rani to inject the Toxic Waste, and neither did she, but she wouldn't back down.

They stood there, staring at each other angrily, when suddenly; a guard fell to the ground. An arrow was in his back. Another fell, and another, before finally, something else fell. A short girl, kind-of pudgy, with fiery red hair. She had cat's ears, and large cat like eyes. She held a bronze knife in her hands. She fell right on top of one of the guards, taking him out in a few seconds. She stood up, holding the knife out in front of her. Ropes fell from the ceiling, and others zipped down from the skylights on the roof. They landed next to her, making three in all. Lucas, Nolan, and Katia, all ready to fight. They stood beside Rani, weapons drawn.

"We got you," Katia whispered, and Rani smiled. Someone had been looking for her.

"What is this?" Valen laughed, the wall of concrete sliding back into the ground. "Three kids? Three children?" He laughed heartily, yet ice was still apart in his voice. "It would take a hundred adult Clessi warriors to have a chance against me, but yet, there you are."

"Jokes on you," Katia called over to him. "I'm half Mutant." She threw her knife, and it zipped through the air so fast that Valen didn't have time to react. It sliced through his sleeve, cutting a deep gash on his arm.

"Enough of this child's play," Valen shouted at them, his voice like an earthquake. "Kill the red haired girl!"

135

Katia gasped, her face going pale. A silver spear was through her stomach, and blood was soaking through her shirt. She turned to look at her killer before she fell. He had short brown hair, bright green eyes, but the smile that was always on his face wasn't there anymore. It was replaced by a grim frown. Lucas pulled his spear out of Katia, who fell to the ground. She was gasping for air now, and there was blood on her lips as she tried to breathe. Nolan ran to her, and grabbed her hand.

"No, please don't Katia," he said, his voice cracking. "Don't you dare." Tears were running down Katia's face, and the blood was staining her lips bright red.

"I'm so sorry," She said to him.

"No!" Nolan cried. "Katia, don't go!"

"I did what I thought was best," Katia chocked out. Rani knew there wasn't much time left for her. The pool of blood was growing larger and larger by the second. Rani didn't know the girl, yet she could feel tears brimming in her eyes, threating to spill over.

"Goodbye, Nolan," Katia whispered. Her eyes were starting to lose their light. "Make sure they all are safe for me," She whispered, and her eyes fluttered shut. Her breathing stopped, and the last tear fell from her eye.

Nolan had a tear running down his face. He leaned over, kissing Katia's forehead gently. He turned to look at Lucas. Lucas held his spear, covered in Katia's blood.

"You traitor!" he roared. "You filthy, murderous, traitor scum! She trusted you!" Nolan sliced at Lucas with his sword, but Lucas dodged every single attempt. He leapt backwards, over twenty feet, landing beside Valen. "Lucas, she trusted you! And you killed her! You killed her!" tears were streaming freely down Nolan's face now, and he held his sword, ready to kill Lucas.

"My name isn't Lucas, you blithering Idiot," he growled. "It's Andrew. Andrew Valen." Sylvia screamed, bursting from her cage and onto the stairs. She ran to stand beside them. Her bow lay beside Katia, at the edge of the pool of scarlet blood. She picked it up, along with her arrows. She fired several at Lucas, or Andrew, whoever he was. Stones flew up, blocking every single one. Sylvia fired nine arrows before she admitted defeat. Tears streamed down her face, but they weren't sad tears. They were tears of anger. She had fury that she had never felt before. She picked up a sword that one of the guards had had and charged at them, but the rocks flew up, slamming her against the metal wall. She fell to the ground, moaning in pain.

"You son of a-" Sylvia started, but Valen cut her off.

"Son of a what?" he said, smiling evilly.

Sylvia opened her mouth, probably to cuss both off them out, but Rani cut them off.

"I may not have known who that girl was. I may not have known who a lot of the people that you have killed where, but I do know this. You will not kill a single one more." She said, clenching the needle tightly in her hand. She threw it at them, but Valen simply caused more rocks to fly up in front of himself and Andrew. The needle shattered, spraying out the blue toxic waste all over the stones.

"And you all are going to stop me?" Valen laughed. "You are all under twenty. Children. Just children! Beating me!"

"Yeah," Nolan said, clenching his sword tightly. He walked a few steps forward, standing right next to Rani. "Yeah, you"

"You and what army?" Valen asked, his tone sinister.

Rani opened her mouth to say something, but at that moment, the wall by the entrance burst open, spewing metal everywhere. Coming through the wall was large Semi, which Rani and Nolan leapt out of the way off. It continued towards Valen and Andrew, and three figures leapt from the driver's seat as Valen made a huge wall of Concrete rise out of the floor, crushing the truck like a tin can.

Garret, Lydia, and Trent rolled away from the Truck, leaping to their feet and standing beside Rani.

Garret gasped. Rani looked different. She was taller. He legs were muscular and strong, and her arms were flexed with rippling muscle and power. Her face was different somehow, more angular and absolutely stunning. Her eyes glowed a kind of unnatural electric blue, as if they weren't real at all, because nothing could look that bright and captivating that was natural. Her face was stern, and her eyebrows were knit together with concern. Electricity flecked over her skin, glowing like a glittering aura around her.

"Rani!" Lydia shouted happily.

"We came to rescue you!" Said Garret, slightly disappointed that she had rescued herself, but he had a big smile across his face.

"Look out!" yelled Nolan, pulling them out of the way as chunks of concrete rubble flew by. The truck fell on its side, and the two villains climbed over.

"A truck, my son, and two random children, that's your army?" Valen asked, laughing. "Are you joking?"

A volley of arrows was launched from the area that Sylvia was in, and then she ran up and joined them. Valen blocked every arrow with a chunk of concrete.

"What's the plan?" She asked, holding her ribs. A small patch of blood had appeared there, and Nolan grabbed her arm, checking her over to make sure she was alright.

"There's no plan," Rani said, ducking as concrete slabs sailed over her head. The ground shook beneath her, and the ground they were standing on started to lift into the air.

"New plan!" said Sylvia, rushing towards the edge.

The rest followed her, stumbling as they lifted higher and higher.

"Jump!" She yelled, leaping off the edge. They all followed, falling several feet before hitting the ground, crumbling to their knees and onto their stomachs.

Rani stood up, electricity flowing around her. It started to turn from blue to a shimmering gold, and she formed a large ball of energy into her hands, but suddenly, she heard Lydia shout.

Rani turned and watched her best friend crumple to the ground. There were several gray dots sticking to her arms. The others started to do the same, and Rani saw that she was surrounded. Superiors, not just guards. They held silver gun-like objects. They shot at Rani, but as they hit her, they expelled a small shock of electricity.

She turned back to Valen. "Really?" she said. "Electricity? To beat electricity?"

"Fight fire with fire?" Valen said, sort of unsure about himself.

"No, I don't think so." Rani said, letting the electricity fly. It shot through several concrete slabs, hitting Valen in the center of his chest. He flew several feet backwards, before rolling against the floor for several feet. He moaned, but didn't even try to get up. He laid there, his eyes clenched closed, and his heart pumping unbelievably, as if he were still being hit with electricity.

Andrew, or Lucas, Leapt at Rani, clenching the spear in his hand, poised to run Rani through. She shot two more electric balls from her hands, missing him the first time, and then hitting him the second. It exploded against his ches, wrapping him in glowing light as it threw him backwards. He fell to the ground, and sunk to his knees, panting, his face turned towards the floor. His hands were over his heart. His face was screwed up in unbelievable pain, and Rani felt her heart skip a beat. She had caused it. She had really hurt someone. Lots of people, actually. Guards, Superiors, and now a teenager. She felt her stomach clench with sickness. She felt as if she might vomit.

"Now look at what you've done!" said the tall doctor, sweeping across the crumbled ground, and over to Andrew. He laid him down on the ground, and stared into his eyes for a few moments. Andrew stopped breathing. Rani let out a small cry. The boy was dead.

"What did you do?" Rani shouted at him. "Did you kill him!"

"You did, I just shortened the time it took for it to take effect. You caused him to go into cardiac arrest."

"A heart attack?" Rani asked weakly, feeling faint. It wasn't depleted energy, however that cause this. It was guilt.

"Yes, the electric shook made his heartbeat irregular, which was going to kill him." The tall man said, striding away briskly, towards Valen. He leaned over him.

"He however," said the tall man, "is in a coma."

Rani backed away, towards her friends. She knelled beside one of them, Lydia. Lydia still had her utility belt on, and Rani slipped the knife out of one of the pockets, and tucked it into Lydia hood. She put a sheath on it, so it wouldn't cut her. She then pretended to be checking on her friend.

Gathering enough electricity to power a small light bulb, Rani shocked her friend gently. It took three shocks to revive Lydia, but Rani put her hand over her friend's mouth. She put her finger to her lip, signaling her to stay quiet. Lydia nodded slightly, then closed her eyes. Rani tapped the knife, and Lydia nodded again.

Rani stood back up, walking towards the tall man.

"What exactly did you do to my friends?" she asked, gathering a large ball of electricity.

"They," The tall man said, motioning to the Superiors that surrounded them, "Used electrical shocks to cause unconsciousness." Rani walked up closer, faster, ready to strike, but the man turned about, holding out the bracelet with the white crystals on it.

"I don't think so," he said, waving it in her face.

"Why aren't they attacking me?" Rani asked, motioning to the superiors surrounding her.

"They all have bracelets off their own. You're trapped," said the tall man, going back to helping Valen, his leader.

"Oh," said Rani stupidly. She looked towards the hole in the wall, where the rain was pouring down. A few Superiors were melding the metal back into place, and a muscular Superior was dragging the crushed Semi out the door. The floor, however, remained ruined, and it probably would until Valen decided to fix it. Rani was pacing back and forth, thinking. Lydia could protect herself, but the others couldn't. *Maybe,* she thought, *if I wake them all up, I can cause a distraction and they'll get away.* She walked over towards them, gathering a small bit of electricity.

Before she got there, though, Rani was grabbed by a Superior with rough skin. The Superior had had skin like metal, cold, smooth, and hard. They pulled her towards a metal door surrounded with crystals. They unlocked the door and shoved her inside.

The room was dark, with dark gray metal walls and floor. There was a bed pushed up against the one wall, and it was really only a small cot with a brown blanket on it.

"Let me out!" yelled Rani, banging her fist against the door. "Let me go!" She held her hand against the door, and she could fell pain as she pushed against it. The crystals were affecting her. Frustrated, she stormed away from the door, leaping back in surprise as she saw another person in the room with her.

Decisions

A tall figure strode strongly up the massive stone stairs that dominated the entryway to the Safe Zone. The weapons were no longer on the walls, they were being used. Every day since the disappearance of Valen's son, the Safe Zone had been under brutal attack by the Superiors, and Mutants alike. It was like they had declared undivided war against them. The ground rolled as an explosion killed more, and the figure on the staircase stumbled.

No one had to tell Jaden she looked different. The first snowflakes had fallen today, yet she wore a black tank top that hugged her top half, showing off her athletic frame. A cut went throw her lips, leaving a thin red line that would scar later. Her arm was wrapped in gauze, but fresh blood soaked through the spot where a dagger had been plunged yesterday.

Her skin was paler than normal, as she hadn't slept well since then. She had been taking on extra shifts, fighting too long. Her jeans were shredded and legs were dotted with bruises and cuts. Her right side was blackened with bruising from being hit with a rock the size of her head. Her hair was knotted and greasy. She fingernails had bllod and dirt caked under them, and sweat glistened over her despite the below freezing temperatures outside. The dagger she always kept with her was deep in the chest of a Superior woman who had run at her, her hands ending in twisted razor sharp claws.

Jaden winced as she made it to the top of the stairs. The sound of battle was roaring outside, but she was in desperate need of a shower and at least six hours of sleep. It was wistful thinking, the water was mainly being used as a weapon. Ice made excellent one time murder weapons that shattered when you tried to pull them back out.

Boiling water was poured off of the roof when Mutants or Superiors got too close. Boiling oil had been used at first, but they had ran out in the first two days.

Sleep was a different story. Everyone roomed with four people in the Safe Zone. Jaden had watched her last surviving roommate be stabbed today during the battle. She had watched the light leave her eyes. The other two had burned to death when a particularly nasty Superior had gone suicidal and blew up a section of the battle, killing three dozen at least. Jaden knew if she slept, she would have nightmares about them.

A noise near her shocked her. She spun around, hands out, fists up, ready to fight with her bare hands.

A boy with mocha colored skin and black hair was stumbling in the doors. He had bright gray eyes, and held his side as it was stained with blood. Jaden ran down the stairs to catch him as he fell forward.

"Henry!" she screamed.

Henry Niles lay in her arms. He moaned.

"I'm fine," he said. He pulled up his shirt, revealing a cut across his side that though it was bleeding, was far from fatal.

Jaden scanned his mind, searching for his doubts his fears. Like his sisters, Henry's mind was all hard logic and knowledge weighed heavily before emotions. He would be fine, he knew the medical field well enough to know that. Jaden sighed in relief.

"Damn Mutant," he moaned. He sat up, leaning against Jaden for support. She felt his blood, sticky on her hands. She read through the memory quickly, and Henry watched her, well aware of what she was doing.

"Damn," she whispered, taking an intake of breathe as she saw what he had gone through today.

"The attacks are getting worse," Henry said, moaning as Jaden helped him to his feet. She lead him down the corridor, toward the overcrowded corridor.

"You don't think I know that?" she said behind gritted teeth. "I watched Sari die today,"

"I'm sorry," said Henry. There was gentleness in his voice that calmed Jaden down. They walked in silence for a while, minus the echoing of their shoes and the sounds of the battle.

"The Council has spoken of doing the X protocol," Henry said after a pause.

Jaden moaned. "Not again. I won't agree."

Henry shifted uneasily. "It has every vote but one."

"My vote." Jaden exclaimed. "Head of the Junior guard."

"Too many have died, Jaden. We don't have another choice anymore."

"But I'm not willing to follow out the Protocol."

"It's not about you," Henry said quietly. Jaden paused. "It's about what's best for all of us. All the Clessi."

"What about Sylvia, and Katia, and the others?" Jaden protested.

"What about everyone here?" Henry spat.

"Lydia will never find us if we go through with it."

So leave a sign.

Jaden jumped back in surprise. The voice was so clear in her head, it was as if Henry had spoken out loud. But she knew he didn't. He had said to leave a sign. That would break protocol. They would be kicked out of the Council.

"How?" She mumbled. She looked around, but no one was around them. They were safe.

The one girl's backpack was recovered. Leave a note. Something to reassure them. Give them hope. They'll need it.

Henry stood up straighter now. They were in front of the infirmary doors. He let go of Jaden, and walked unevenly inside. Jaden stood still, stunned.

Leaving a note would break Council law.

Jaden walked calmly up the stairs, her mind buzzing.

Leaving a note could put everyone in a lot of danger.

Sylvia's room was unlocked. Katia never locked it; and the other two girls in it were dead now. They would be heartbroken when they got back. If they lived.

Leaving a note was against protocol.

Jaden scribbled quickly and shoved the paper in the bag.

The Council was mostly empty when Jaden ran in. It was a large rectangle room, filled with a huge mahogany table and dozens of chairs for each Council member. Only the Head of the Trainee Guard and Secretary of Quests and Rescues were in there. The secretary hardly looked up, and was instead writing something down frantically, as if they thought they had seconds left. Jaden walked up to her spot at the table.

"I cast my vote for the good of the Clessi under our supervision." Jaden boomed, her voice echoing around the room, startling even her. She took a deep breath. She was ready. She could do it. Even though she hated what this meant.

"I, Jaden Hallow, vote yes to the X Protocol. I vote yes to the destruction of the North East branch of the Safe Zone."

It was said like a death sentence, like Jaden had just condemned an innocent man to die for the sins of others. In a way, she had.

Samantha

"Hello," Said the person, a small girl with long blonde hair. Her eyes were wide, and one was bright, forest green, and the other was a pale, sickly yellow, like a hawks. She wore a purple shirt and a little jean skirt, both faded and old. She sat on the floor, a tattered doll in her hands. Rani gasped. *This was Garret's little sister,* she thought, *It must be.*

"Hello," said Rani, sitting cross legged on the floor. "What's your name?"

"Samantha Valen." She said sweetly. *She must be on her angelic side*, Rani realized.

"I'm Rani. Rani McSean," She said, biting her lip. They sat in silence for a minute. "I know your brother," Rani said, after what felt like a year.

"Which one?" said the girl, clutching the doll. It was a rag doll, with brown yarn hair, and a long red fabric stripped dress, which was torn in several spots. The doll had teeth marks, as if a dog had bitten it several times, and stuffing peeked out from some holes in the doll.

"Garret," Rani said, not willing to tell her about Andrew.

"Gary did make it safely, then?" Samantha said, smiling. Rani winced slightly at the sight of the little girl's razor sharp fang-like teeth.

"Yes," she said. "He brought me with him,"

"Is he out there with my Dad?" she asked, her face suddenly sad. Rani nodded, looking guiltily at the ground. It was her fault they were all were here, after all. If she had just been able to run a little bit faster, maybe she wouldn't have been kidnapped and none of this would have ever happened.

"What about Andrew?" she asked, hiding behind her doll.

"He's out there too," Rani said, and Samantha's eyes widened even more.

"I don't think he'll hurt Garret," Rani said quickly, and Samantha looked relived.

"You're like me, aren't you?" asked Samantha, reaching out and grabbing Rani's hand. "You're special too."

"Yes, I am," said Rani.

"Why don't you have lines all over you too?" asked Samantha, and Rani was confused until she realized that she meant the veins.

"The tall man in the white lab coat gave me some sort of medicine," said Rani. The girl smiled, and Rani couldn't help but smile back, even though the teeth were freaking her out.

"The man told me the oldest I'll ever get is twelve,"

Samantha said. "How old are you?"

"I'm fifteen," Rani said.

"I knew it!" exclaimed Samantha. "I knew he was lying!" Rani didn't have the heart to tell her that he probably wasn't lying. Samantha didn't look very healthy right now. Her skin was gray, and the blackish blue veins looked enlarged and swollen.

"How old are you now?" Rani asked

"I'm seven," Samantha said, smiling. Rani's heart broke a little bit. If she looked so sick now, she couldn't even imagine how sick she would be when she was eleven.

"How long have you been in here?" Rani asked, changing the subject.

"A week or two. Gary had left two weeks before Dad came home one day. He was angry. He hit Mommy, and took me away." The girl began to get a faraway look in her eye, and Rani feared that her split personality was about to change.

Samantha doubled over in pain for a second, and then looked up. Rani gasped. Her eyes were both neon blue now, the same color as Rani's.

"Who are you?" Samantha asked. Rani explained quickly. Samantha set the doll down and walked over towards the door.

"What are you doing?" Rani asked.

"Same thing I've been doing for a week and a half. It'll go faster with our combined strength." The girl began to pull at the door, making the hinges stretch a tiny bit. Rani helped her, and the hinges moved a tiny bit more. Rani pulled with all her might, but the hinges held strong.

"The crystals drain physical energy as well," Samantha explained, pulling harder at the door. "You have to be two or more feet away to be at full strength."

"What if one of us pulls at the door, and the other stands two feet away and pulls at the other person?" Rani asked. Samantha smiled.

"That could work!" She exclaimed, grinning. Rani laughed. Samantha had the same quirky grin that Garret always had.

"Come on, time's wasting," said Rani.

A Real Nightmare

Lydia had lain very still when the men had transferred her. She had lain still when she had been locked in the cage. But she would not lie still as they tried to drag her away to be experimented on. She sat up quickly, taking the tall man in the lab coat and the metal skinned Superior who was dragging her quite a scare.

"Let me go," She said, looking directly into the metal skinned man's eyes. He nodded slowly, stupidly, like a brainwashed child.

"Focus, you blithering idiot!" snapped the tall man, hitting the metal skinned man on the back of the head. Lydia lost eye contact, and the connection was broken. The metal skinned Superior began dragging her by the leg again. She reached around and tapped whatever Rani had hidden in her hood. The utility belt had been taken away when they had looked her in the cage, but the metal object in the hood hadn't been touched. Lydia couldn't figure out what it was though, and she didn't want to give away the trick up her sleeve just yet.

She was dragged out of the cage, onto a staircase she hadn't seen from the cage, and onto the broken concrete ground. There was no sign of Valen or Andrew, and Lydia didn't want to know where they were. She grabbed a loose chunk of rubble and tucked it quickly in her gray wool coat's big pocket. Neither the tall man nor the metal skinned Superior noticed, and so Lydia stuffed another chunk in the other pocket. She could probably take the tall man, and brainwash the metal skinned man. She felt a twinge of guilt at the thought of controlling someone, but she shook it away. She had to do this. There was no other choice.

As she was dragged, her mind wandered. Was her book still dry in her backpack? They had left their bags on the boat, in a cupboard that they hadn't known was there. They also hadn't known about the small cabin under the deck. It was very small, only about five feet by six, and it was mostly just a cushion that spanned the whole way. There were cupboards that were closed with a latch, sunk into the wall so there was more room. It was dry down there, and Lydia wished she had known about it earlier that day. She wondered if she would ever see the boat again.

She was dragged past a metal door with white crystals lining it. She could have sworn the door opened just a crack, opening inwards a tiny bit, but she shook off the thought. The door was three inches thick, with huge cast iron locks on the outside. No one was getting out of there.

Lydia was dragged into the small room, and strapped to a chair. She looked around. The room was blindingly white. There was nothing dirty in the room, and it was as brilliantly white as the tall man's lab coat.

She watched as the man took something out of a silver metal box. It was some kind of silver liquid. She looked at the label, but all she could make out was a capital B on the side. He filled a syringe with the strange liquid, and then walked over to Lydia. He cleaned her arm with an alcohol wipe. The wipe was freezing, and gave Lydia goose bumps all over her body. The tall man was about to inject the liquid when someone, a superior guard of some kind, rushed into the room. The whispered something in the tall man's ear, and he nodded and set the syringe down without injecting Lydia at all. The tall man strode out of the room.

"Watch her," The tall man in the white lab coat ordered the metal-skinned man. He nodded. The second the tall man had closed the door to the room, Lydia fixed her round gray eyes on the Superior. He looked into her eyes, and he was a goner.

Lydia's eyes were large, gray eyes flecked with silver and iridescent highlights, and anyone who looked into them stared in awe. This played to her advantage, since eye contact was required to use her ability.

"Untie me," she said, twisting her voice to sound commanding but not overbearing. She didn't want to overpower the superior. She didn't want to destroy him using this power.

"Okay," the man mumbled, tripping over the words, stumbling and slurring them as if he were drunk. He undid the latches on her binds, and she rubbed the alcohol off her arm.

"Listen to me very carefully. I need you to forget my face, and then go to sleep for a while, okay?" She said, and the man nodded before falling against the wall and sliding to the floor. Lydia smiled at him, a crooked, sad smile, feeling guilty already. He would probably be in a lot of trouble for this. He might even get beaten. The tall man was certainly cruel, and Lydia didn't want to underestimate him.

She grabbed the object out of her hood, and found it was her knife, sheathed. Lydia slid the sheath off, and tucked it into her pocket, next to the rubble. Lydia searched the room over quickly, looking for her utility belt. She didn't find it, and as she heard footsteps approaching the room, she crawled into the white cabinet under the sink, thanking her lucky stars that she was scrawny and the cabinet was only half filled. She heard the door swing open, and the tall man exclaimed in surprise. He cursed a few times, then she heard him kick the metal-skinned the man, and she could hear the dull ring his skin gave off. The metal skinned-man awoke with a start, started to say something, but the tall man cut him off.

Lydia couldn't hear the words the tall man was saying, because they were muffled and blended together through the pressed wood that made up the cabinet. She heard someone yelling, then she heard the buckles being locked on the table. She squeezed up close to the crack in the cupboard, looking through it and out into the room. One of the boys that had been fighting Valen with her, one of the boys who had gone on the quest to save Rani and the others-which meant his name was either Lucas or Nolan, if her memory served her correctly- was being strapped to the chair. Every fiber in Lydia's heart and brain told her to jump right out of the cupboard and save the boy, but her body was frozen up in fear. Tears started running silently down her face, and she couldn't even wipe them away out of fear that someone would hear her. She closed her eyes as she heard the boy start to scream, and then, the tall man backed up into the counter top she was hidden under. Lydia heard the restrains snapping, and then the tall man cried out in fear. He had done something very, very wrong to the boy. She heard a scream of pain from the tall man, and then she heard him fall backwards against the floor, and she heard a strangled gasping, as if something was trying to stop itself from crying out. It was a sound that made Lydia scared beyond measure

Lydia had the bravery to open her eyes for a second, and she peeked outside of the cabinet door. The boy was standing up. His skin was pale, nearly as white as the room, but his eyes were pitch black, all black, and Lydia feared if she looked at them for more than a second she would surely be sucked inside, like a black hole. The boy had blood on his hands, yet he held no weapons. He had a crazed look on his face, and Lydia closed her eyes and held her breath. Her heart beat loud and heavy in her chest, and she feared that he would hear it, but she heard heavy footsteps leaving the room. The door closed, and she could hear muffled screams from outside.

Timidly, Lydia pushed open the cabinet door. She crawled outside of it and looked around the room. The restraints were snapped roughly, as if they had been torn by brute strength alone. She turned and let out a gasp and a sob. The tall man laid on the floor, his head propped up

159

against the wall. His eyes were closed, and his starched white lab coat was stained with blood, blood that was also spattered across the cabinet. His face was scratched, and bloody, as well as his chest was. His hand still clutched the syringe, which held a tiny bit of liquid still. The liquid was gold, and Lydia turned the Syringe around, Gasping as she read the name. Nightmare blood. The boy was now a nightmare. One of the things that she had read about in her classes. But that was impossible! They had killed the last one nearly a hundred years ago! *But what if it was true?* Lydia thought. Loose, in a building with hundreds of Clessi. Lydia began to sob. Screams outside continued, and Lydia leaned against the door. There was no way she was leaving this room. She fumbled at the doorknob, locking it. She slid down the door until she was sitting. She then buried her face in her hands, sobbing.

Sacrifices

Sylvia had just woken up when Nolan left the room. She sighed in relief. He was alive. She had been afraid she would lose him as well. She had been afraid. Then she saw him. His skin, his eyes, and her heart stopped beating for a moment. She watched him murder a guard, without a weapon. She saw his eyes. They weren't Nolan's eyes. They were the eyes of a cold blooded killer. A Nightmare. The only person she had left from her quest was a Nightmare. She had read the stories. They didn't have happy endings. Sylvia sat up, tears running down her face. She wiped them away. She wasn't going to cry. She was going to be brave. She had always been brave, and if she was to die, she would face it without fear, without tears, and without regrets. Her heart may have been broken, her life doomed, and lost everyone she cared about, but she would not let it show. She would die bravely.

Her sister. What about her sister? Was she dead? Sylvia looked franticly around the cages, looking for her sister's face. She didn't see her anywhere. Was it possible she was already dead? She had seen her earlier, when she was fighting. She had been there then, but she had been two focused on fighting to run to her little sister and tell her that everything would be alright, that she was there for her. Sylvia closed her eyes, breathing heavily and shakily, trying to keep her composure. If there was a chance she could save her sister, then she had to do it. Sylvia put her hand on the cage door, holding a small metal item in her hand. It was a small necklace. She jammed it into the lock, twisting it and turning it, wincing as she heard the metal scrapping together. The lock clicked, and Sylvia leapt into the air and onto the staircase she knew was there. She landed heavily, and gasped heavily. Her side burned, and she looked down to see that the patch of blood had grown bigger. She grunted as she stood up, and started running down the stairs. She grabbed a sword off the ground, ignoring the patch of blood it laid in.

Nolan was injured, a long scratch across his chest, gushing blood. The sight off the scarlet liquid made Sylvia sick and weak, but she pushed the thought away. He felled another Superior, and turned to gaze upon the carnage he had done. Dozens of guards lay on the floor, and Sylvia knew they were dead. So many innocent lives had been lost, no, not innocent, but lives had still been lost, so many lives, and no matter what kind of person they were, that didn't make that right. She clenched the sword tightly, her knuckles turning white from the effort. Nolan turned to look at her. She saw a single tear run down his face, a black tear, and she saw fear on his face. It didn't matter that he was different now, he was still the Nolan she knew. His mouths formed some word, and as he ran forward, his hands stretched forward, trying to kill her for sure, she realized he had mouthed please. She raised her sword, tears stinging her eyes, but not spilling over. He got closer and closer, and Sylvia prepared herself.

This was it. This was the end.

*   *   *

Rani and Samantha had heard the screams outside. They were soft through the heavy door, but they could hear them. They decided to wait it out. If something was hurting the people out there, they might just want to wait. Samantha had turned into full mutant, her eyes burning red, tearing at the doll, ripping new holes in the dress and fabric. She had thrown herself at the door, until finally, she had turned back into the first girl, the human. Her eyes were green and yellow again, and Rani held her, the sobbing child, in her arms, rocking her back and forth gently, whispering gentle words to calm her down.

Samantha could hear the screams. She was terrified. She missed her Mom and her brother, and she was horrified that her brother could be out there, hurt. Her doll was torn and beaten more again, and she knew the monster had gotten out again. She didn't remember being the monster, or the other girl, but she knew she became them sometimes. She sobbed into Rani's shoulder as Rani calmed her down. Rani was like the sister she had never had.

After a few more minutes, everything went quiet. So very quiet that it scared the two of them. Rani stood up and walked over to the door, pressing her ear to it. It was quiet outside, and Rani put her hands on the door, and pulled with a burst of strength. It pulled the hinges a bit more, and Rani gave one final yank, and it opened up. Samantha stood behind Rani, clinging onto her leg.

Rani scoped Samantha up into her arms and carried her outside. Samantha clung to the doll and Rani, burying her head into Rani's shoulder. The scene was gruesome. Blood and Superiors were everywhere. The people in cages were fine, shaken, but fine. Rani ran over to a person lying on the ground, still breathing. She set Samantha down, and Samantha sat, her knees pulled up to her chest and her head buried into her knees. The doll was clutched tightly, and stuffing leaked from a new hole.

Rani knelled next to the girl. She was tall, with extraordinarily long legs. Her hair was long and curly, and light brown. It was braided to the side loosely. The girl opened her eyes, and Rani looked down into her cobalt blue eyes.

Rani recognized her as the girl with the bow from earlier. The girl looked weakly up at her. Her throat was covered in blood, as was her stomach.

"Rani?" she got out, her voice weak.

"How do you know my name?" Rani asked, looking at the girl curiously.

"How could I forget the name of my little sister?" The girl said, with a smile. Rani gasped. She could feel her throat seem to shrink, and her breathing became forced and difficult.

"S. A. M." She said, pulling the necklace out. The girl pulled out her own, gold as well. It had R. E. M. carved into it. The girl let out a weak smile.

"Sylvia Anna McSean. She said. Rani felt tears running down her face, and Sylvia shook her head. "Don't cry. I waited for years, how many years, eight?"

"Ten," said Rani.

"Ten years. I've waited for ten years just to see my little sister make it to the Safe Zone. And now you will, because of what I did today. Just make sure it wasn't in vain, okay?" Rani started to sob, holding her big sister's hand. Sylvia took a necklace out of her pocket, and handed it to Rani. It was a silver lightning bolt, with the same inscription on it. The edges were rough and sanded down, and it had a few small scratches across it, but it shone like a mirror. Rani clutched it in her hand tightly, so tight that the edges cut into her hands. She slipped t over her head and onto her neck, and it dangled on her neck, along with her locket and her own lightning bolt.

"Tell the Safe Zone goodbye for me," Sylvia said, and Rani held her hand, crying, until Sylvia's breathing stopped. After several minutes, Samantha walked over to Rani, who was still on her knees. Samantha wrapped her arms around Rani, hugging her.

"It's ok," She whispered. Rani sobbed as she hugged Samantha, and Samantha cried too. They sat there, crying for a while, until a sudden noise made them both turn their heads. Lydia pocked her head out of the white room. Rani stood up, wiping her wet eyes. She gripped Samantha's hand, and Samantha gripped hers. Lydia ran over to her best friend and wrapped her in a tight hug. Rani hugged her back, dropping Samantha's hand for a minute as she hugged her.

"I never thought I was going to see you again," said Lydia.

"I never thought I would see you again either," Rani said, her voice breaking.

They broke the hug, and Rani grabbed Samantha's hand again. Lydia looked curiously at her, and Rani shrugged.

"It's Garret's little sister, Samantha." She said, looking around the room.

"Garret never told me he had a sister," Lydia mumbled, but Rani didn't hear her.

"Where do you think the keys to this are?" Rani asked, pointing to the changes.

"I don't know." Admitted Lydia, a sentence she rarely said. They searched for several minutes before they found them, along with their weapons. Rani didn't need one. She was a weapon.

They unlocked every cage, helping every person down the staircase. They would have to find a way to get every single one of them to the Safe Zone somehow. Rani forgot all of that as she saw Garret's face though, as they unlocked his cage. He scooped up his little sister, spinning her around and around, holding her tightly, and in that moment, Rani knew what love looked like. She smiled. When Garret set her down, he grabbed her and pulled her into a tight embrace. He swept her off her feet, spinning her around like he had with his sister.

"We're alive!" he said, joy in his voice.

"Yeah," said Rani, her voice suddenly hollow and empty.

Garret looked confused for a moment, and Lydia looked at him, mouthing to him. He gasped, and drew Rani into another bear hug, rubbing her back soothingly. A few tears ran down her face, soaking into the shoulder of his shirt. They stood there, hugging for a few minutes, Until Samantha pulled on Garret's shirt.

"Gary?" She said.

"Yeah?" he asked, taking all his willpower to break the hug.

"Did you see that guy?"

"What guy?" He asked, knelling beside her.

"The one who just ran out of the building over there," She said, pointing her finger towards an exit.

"What did he look like?"

"He was tall, with a lab coat, but it was all bloody. His face was all torn up, too."

Lydia gasped, backing up. Her hand covered her mouth, and her round eyes were wide.

"I thought he was dead!" she said. "That whole time in that room, I thought he was dead over there, and he was really alive, and watching me and-" Lydia started to hyperventilate, and Rani held her best friends hand.

"It's ok," she said. "It might not have been him."

"But what if it was?"

"Then we'll just have to look out for horribly scarred, bloody, tall men wearing lab coats. Lydia, he'll end up in the hospital, where they'll test his blood type, and the Trailers will get him." Garret said. Lydia shivered at the name Trailers, and he shot her an apologetic look.

"Let's free the rest of them," said Rani, motioning to the other cages. Samantha held Rani's hand with one hand and Garret's with the other. They smiled at each other, and Rani wiped the tears from her eyes with her other hand. She would have to learn how to be brave like her sister was. She would have to. There was no other choice. Not anymore.

They opened up the cages, every one. They freed over a hundred Clessi. They all stumbled weakly to the ground, weak and injured.

"What do we do know?" Rani thought out loud, and Lydia looked over at her.

"Well, first things first." She began. "We need to feed them. They look like it's been a week since they've had any food or water."

The group, now including Trent once again, searched the warehouse. They found where everything was stored; the food, the weapons, and more keys. They grabbed it all, not knowing what these keys were for. They passed out as much food as they could. Rani gulped down as much food as she could. She had forgotten how long she had been without food.

They sat around, watching all the weak children and teenagers around them eat and regain a little bit of their strength. Rani looked down at Samantha, who sat in Garret's lap. She smiled, through tears still burned in her eyes. She squeezed the lightning bolt necklaces around her neck. They clicked together, and Rani realized they were different sizes. They fit together, facing opposite directions, forming a heart with squared edges. Rani breathed heavily, feeling more tears rising to her face. It was as if that her dad had known that one girl would end up having the necklaces. He had known that only one could have survived. He must have always known. Maybe Sylvia had figured out that when she was eight, and that had been the spark behind her running away. Now she would never know.

Rani let go of them, and they stayed in the heart shape, connected. Rani wiped tears of her eyes and cheeks with the back of her hand.

Lydia was studying the keys in her hands. She ran her fingers over them, reading the tiny carving on the front.

"Garret, come look at this," she said. Garret lifted Samantha off his lap and handed her to Rani. Samantha, fast asleep, lay in Rani's lap, holding the doll close to her chest.

"What is it?" Garret asked, looking at the key.

"There are vehicle keys," Lydia said.

"So?" he said, leaning against the wall.

"So, I know how we are getting out of here," She said, standing up. Ranis stood up, shifting Samantha so that she could carry her and walk. Garret walked over to Rani and lifted Samantha gently out of her arms and into his.

They started walking towards the large group of Clessi out in front of them, and told them one by one where they were going. Walking outside, they were met by frigid air, and a light rain. The swirling clouds above them had stopped. The major storm had passed, and now, all that left was to withstand the rest of the storm. They weren't quite out of the storm yet, and for all they knew, they could be standing in the eye of the storm, and the worst was still yet to come, but they didn't care. They had each other, and for the moment it was all the mattered.

They walked around the building. From the outside, you couldn't see the horrors that had happened within. They walked through the rain, letting it was away the memory of what they had seen inside. All the horror, and the blood, they just let it be rinsed away, tucking it as far away into their memories as possible. The found the vehicles. They were big, white vans with no windows. They were labeled for different things, fake companies, with make-believe phone numbers and logos printed on them. Lydia unlocked one with her key, one decorated with the logo of a fake plumbing company, and slid open the door. The van was blank inside, with no seats in the back. Weapons were strapped to the walls, giving it a creepy look in the darkness. Trent stepped into the van first, and started prying the weapons off the walls. He threw them out the door, save for their own.

"Much better," he said. Lydia passed out the keys, and the others did the same. While Lydia went to explain where the safe zone was, Rani and Garret lay Samantha down in the van. Trent climbed in the front.

"Um, Trent, no offence, but I thought you said you couldn't drive?" said Garret.

"Can you drive?" Trent asked a sly smile across his face. Garret shook his head no, and so Trent buckled himself in. After a few minutes, Lydia returned, sliding into the front seat. She buckled herself in, and closed the door.

"They know where to go," said Lydia, "and if not, then that's too bad for them. We gave them all weapons and a means of getting to the Safe Zone. We can't choose for them."

Trent started the car. The engine came to life, and the van shook gently. The interior grew warmer, and Rani felt the warmth fill her body. Her gray sweater hadn't been keeping her very warm, and the heating in the van was very nice. She looked over at Garret, who had Samantha's head in his lap. He was looking down at her, and the little doll clutched in her hands. It was tattered, torn, much like the girl was. He held a small hand, a small, gray hand, with blackish blue veins showing out from the skin, in his own hand. Rani smiled a small sort of smile, more out of hope than out of happiness or amusement.

Trent began to drive, and though he certainly wasn't an experienced driver, they weren't killed in car accident, and that was good enough for the reluctant passengers.

They pulled through the city streets, and Rani noticed out the window how dark it was outside, even though it was only raining lightly outside.

"What time is it?" Rani asked, and Garret looked down at his watch.

"11:37," He said, and Rani sighed, running her fingers loosely through her curly hair. It was tangled, probably since she hadn't really been combing it for the past few days. They drove on in silence for a few minutes, and then the van slowed to a stop. Rani looked out the window. She could see the water, and a bunch of boats bobbing gently in the surf.

"Why are we here?" she asked, and Trent and Lydia opened their doors.

"The docks," Trent said. He slammed his door, and he and Lydia walked off somewhere that Rani couldn't see.

"Why are we at the docks?" asked Rani, confused.

"It's a long story," Garret said. Samantha stirred, and so they stayed quiet for a few minutes in Lydia and Trent's absence. Samantha went back to sleep, and Rani sighed.

"It's so late" she whispered, "but I don't think I can ever sleep again."

"Why not?" Garret asked.

"All the things I've seen, all the people-"she faltered, "The people I've seen die, caused to die, I just don't think-" her voice cracked, and she looked at Garret, her eyes wide and helpless. For a moment, her eyes looked like Samantha's; wide, scared, and weary after seeing too much.

Garret reached out and laced his fingers with hers. She looked at him in surprise, and he smiled, but this time, it wasn't a mischievous smile. It was a sweet, safe smile that made Rani feel warm inside again.

Garret and Lydia returned to the truck, holding loads of

stuff. They slid the back door open, and set their bags down. They slid in a large cushion, and it covered half of the room in the back. The cushion was a few inches thick, and light tan. Garret laid Samantha down on it, and she rolled over, snuggling into it.

They set Garret's backpack down in it as well, and then closed the back door loudly. Samantha stirred again, but quickly fell back into a deep sleep. Garret unzipped his bag with his free hand, and pulled out a blanket. He draped it over Samantha.

Trent and Lydia climbed in the front of the van, and the vehicle restarted. Trent pulled out of the area unevenly, running over a curb with a large bump.

"Where are we going now?" asked Rani quietly, so she wouldn't wake Samantha. "Back to the Safe Zone?"

Trent nodded. "The second star to the right," he said.

"And straight on till morning," Lydia finished, "or probably tomorrow evening. Michigan is a long ways away." Rani smiled, and Garret squeezed her hand gently.

"You two should probably try to get some sleep." Said Trent.

"Why?" Garret teased. "You don't want us to take over driving?"

"I value my life over your feelings," Trent said. "*Please* don't drive and end my life."

"Sleep it is," Garret said, flopping back onto the cushion. Rani lay back, staring at the ceiling. She and Garret were still holding hands. Images from the day flooded back into her mind, but she pushed them away and closed her eyes. She was asleep within seconds. She slept soundly, until halfway through the night, she started to jerk, and shake.

Rani sat up quickly, her body soaked in sweat. Garret was next to her, and he sat up, looking at her in surprise. Tears were running down her face, and he reached out, letting go off her hands. He brought her into a gentle hug, breathing soft words into her ear. He rocked her back and forth gently, as fat, heavy tears ran down her face.

"It's ok," he said. "It was only a dream. It was only a nightmare."

She sobbed into his shoulder. No one else heard them that night. Lydia and Samantha were fast asleep. Trent had ear buds in his ears, listening to the radio.

Rani fell back asleep in Garret's arms, and he laid her down gently. He covered her with his jacket, and before he went back to sleep, he kissed her forehead gently. Her eyelids fluttered, but she didn't wake up. He lay down, holding her hand, falling asleep with a smile on his face.

The Safe Zone

It was late afternoon when Rani finally woke up. Everyone else was awake; everyone but she, and she sat up, rubbing the sleepiness from her eyes.

"We made great time last night," said Lydia from the driver's seat. Trent sat on the passenger side, eating from a fast food bag. Garret handed her a bag, and Rani could smell the fries inside. "We should be there in about an hour,"

Rani opened the bag, scarfing down the food. She ate everything, even the cold, greasy fries that had fallen to the bottom of the bag. The radio was on quietly, and Lydia turned it up. It was a song they all knew vaguely. Garret was the first to start singing. Everyone but Samantha started singing soon after, but Samantha laughed her heart out. The van was all smiles and laughs, and it stayed that way, even as it bumped along the gravel on the side of the train tracks. They drove up to the short section of woods, and found a path that had been used two or three times earlier. They drove through, and the atmosphere in the van disappeared. They stopped the van, and Rani leapt out the back door.

"Oh my God," Lydia said, stepping out of the van. Rani ran towards the brick wall, the one that Jaden had been sitting on when they had first arrived. Rani had never met Jaden, but she remembered the blond girl who had helped Garret and Lydia get to safety. That wall was now the only thing still standing. The whole place was a little more than dust. She climbed over the wall and ran into the area.

The wind whistled high and loud, screaming in the girl's ears as she sat down on the rubble. Dust and ash covered everything around her, and she began to sob as she looked around. They really were alone now. Where had everything gone so wrong? She had finally found a place where she belonged, after waiting so long, and now it was gone, snatched away. Hot, heavy tears rolled down her cheeks, warming her frozen cheeks which stung in the cold air. She buried her face in her hands, not knowing what else to do. What else could she do? She had lost everything now, and her heart ached.

Garret ran up behind her. He set his hand on her shoulder. She covered her mouth with her hand, trying to keep the sobs from sounding, while fat, heavy tears ran down her face. There was no sign of people, or Clessi anywhere. No sign of any battle. It was as if the whole place had simply been empty, and then blown to kingdom come.

Trent gasped. "No, NO!"

The others looked at him. He only shook his head, murmuring something about protocols.

"Rani?" Lydia called. "You might want to see this." Rani wiped off her face, and walked over to where Lydia was standing. Sitting there, on the brick wall, was her backpack. It wasn't damaged, not even wet, but was covered in a thin layer of dust and ash.

She opened it up, and inside, on top of all of her stuff, was a piece of paper.

"What does it say?" Lydia asked. Rani looked out over the trees and the mountain in the distance. She had a faraway look in her eyes. She wasn't looking at any of them, but past them, to a place none of them could see. The paper fluttered to the ground, and Rani started to speak after what seemed like a year.

"You are not alone.

Come find us when you're ready."

ABOUT THE AUTHOR

Strange Occurrences is the first published work by Sarah
Elizabeth. Sarah is an avid reader and writer who looks
forward to many more books.

Made in the USA
Middletown, DE
22 August 2015